THE OTHER SIDE OF THE COIN

Other Books by Pierre Boulle

THE BRIDGE OVER THE RIVER KWAI

NOT THE GLORY

FACE OF A HERO

THE TEST

Pierre Boulle

THE OTHER SIDE
OF THE COIN

Translated from the French

by Richard Howard

The Vanguard Press, Inc., New York

"The Spirit bloweth where it listeth"

JOHN, 3: VIII

PART ONE

1   At the edge of the jungle, crouching beside the path that bounded the Kebun Besar plantation, Sen, soldier of the Liberation, began to feel the night's dampness through his clothes. He looked at the sky above the rubber trees and felt relieved that no paleness in the east betrayed the dawn. He cupped his hands around his mouth and gave the signal again. Then he listened, frowning, his head cocked; but no corresponding sound came in reply.

The moment he heard the bushes rustling on the other side of the path Sen stiffened, his fingers tightening around his machine gun. But almost immediately his features relaxed into a grin; a snort had reassured him, and soon the two dark creatures came into view, a swarm of indistinct smaller forms in their wake. It was a family of wild pigs trotting along the path into the jungle.

Sen's eyes flashed in the darkness. Once again his hands tightened on the weapon; here, within arm's reach, was enough meat to feed himself and the comrades in camp for several days. But Kim's orders had been strict: he was not to fire unless in actual danger. For a moment he thought of saying a boar had charged him, that he had fired in self-defense; but Kim knew better than to swallow such a story. Sen lowered his machine gun. He was trying to console himself by observing the creatures' antics when the signal was given some distance away. He listened carefully, answered, and stood up.

There was a sudden noise of hoofbeats and a violent churning in the bushes. Sen gave a start and instinctively leaped back. He had forgotten the wild pigs that had just plunged into the jungle, terrified by his sudden appearance. He immediately recognized the source of the disturbance, shrugged his shoulders, crossed the path, and approached a rubber tree at the foot of which he could distinguish a human figure.

It was a Chinese who worked in one of the plantation stores. The man was not used to night missions and was shaking with fear. Contemptuous of such cowardice, Sen did not bother to reassure him and interrogated him harshly.

"All right. The payroll?"

"It's coming today. The white devil telephoned the bank yesterday."

"What time?"

"Three o'clock, in front of the main office."

Sen decided he had just time enough to reach camp and tell Kim and the comrades, when the sound of a motor broke the silence and a beam of light swept across the rubber trees. The two Chinese did not wait for the car to round the bend. The clerk ran back into the plantation; Sen crossed the path in one leap and disappeared into the jungle as instinctively and as rapidly as the pigs. He was just in time. The jeep had turned onto the road, lighting up the red earth ahead.

Kebun Besar was a plantation like many others in Malaya: a microcosm of several thousand acres lying across a region of steep hills, surrounded on all sides by the jungle, inhabited by black Tamil field hands and yellow Chinese artisans, controlled by three or four sunburned Europeans, and administered by certain far-off paler creatures haunting the City in London or the Bourse in Paris.

Kebun Besar had survived two wars, virulent malaria attacks, whatever damage all the beasts of the jungle could inflict on its trees, and the perpetual speculations of Finance as to the future of the white product that flowed drop by drop early every morning from those same trees. Like its sister plantations, Kebun Besar had been threatened in recent years by a new danger: Chinese terrorism.

The jungle, of which the planters of earlier periods had scarcely been aware—the population of a planet is not conscious of the infinite space surrounding it—had revealed itself as the lair of creatures dangerous in a very different way from elephants or tigers. The latter had certain elementary ambitions—young trees, young cattle—and the havoc they wrought was quickly repaired. But terrorism was directed against the plantation as a whole—it attacked its essence and its principles as an absolute enemy, focusing every effort on the total destruction of the organism. Although it could manifest itself, at irregular intervals, by violent actions against the human or vegetable capital of the plantation, terrorism's most formidable weapon was of a spiritual nature: hatred, the implacable hatred disseminated from a thousand centers in the jungle, spreading its miasma over the entire peninsula until, on certain days, the very air was too dense, too deadly for Western lungs to breathe.

Nevertheless, Kebun Besar took more effective measures against terrorism than many other plantations. To its aggressive manifestations the plantation opposed the energy and experience of its manager, Bernard Delavigne, a Frenchman who after twenty years in Malaya knew virtually every pitfall the Chinese were capable of setting. He protected himself against them with great courage, sometimes even taking the offensive on his own, not hesitating to attack, with the assistance of Rawlinson, the district chief of police and a friend to all planters. As for the terrorist hatred, against which no material weapon was of any avail, at Kebun Besar it found a worthy adversary in Patricia, Bernard's American wife.

Bernard had brought her from the United States after he had spent a long leave of absence there. The marriage had provoked various reactions in the district. At the planters' club, where he was a frequent guest, Rawlinson, whenever the subject came up, never failed to declare that such leaves—though rare events for Occidentals in Malaya—were always occasions for disaster: gambling debts, cirrhosis of the liver (miraculously avoided below the equator), even worse. Assuming a thoughtful expression, he almost always added that there were exceptions to the rule, and that occasionally the six months' vacation was used to good advantage— as in the choice of a respectable wife, the establishment of a household. What Rawlinson really thought was difficult to determine; he was accustomed to look for the truth behind a number of contradictions.

In any case, that was how Kebun Besar had survived until now. In this artificial world created and sustained in the heart of the jungle for a well-defined, concrete purpose, feelings and passions unconnected with the production of rubber could dawn and develop as accessory matters.

This morning Bernard Delavigne was checking on the field hands with a young assistant who had arrived three days before from France—a man named Remy, who was staring at this unknown Malaya with astonished eyes. Bernard was driving the armored jeep himself. Each of them had a machine gun. The manager's jaw tightened as soon as they began driving along the edge of the jungle, and he pressed harder on the accelerator.

"Is that the jungle?" Remy asked.

Bernard was in a bad humor—primarily because he considered it his duty as a manager to be surly with beginners, and also because he had gotten up two hours earlier than usual. It was an act of charity to set the young man's feet on the right path, when he could just as well have assigned the job to his other assistant, Robert Jourdain; but, all the same, he resented the newcomer a little. He didn't like that earnest tone in which Remy had said "the jungle." He asked him in a harsh voice whether he wasn't being a little romantic, or perhaps just feeble-minded: there had been one assistant—

one of the first—who had not been able to get used to this overpowering mass constantly beside him. . . . Bernard had had to send him back to Europe eight days after his arrival—or else, he added casually, the man would have died of melancholia.

"It doesn't affect me that way at all," Remy protested. "I think I'd like to work my way into that labyrinth and explore it. . . ."

This drew a new rebuff. The manager pointed out dryly that the Company had not hired him as an explorer. On his leaves, of course, he was free to do as he liked. "Only," Bernard continued, "you have one bad precedent: Holmes—an English boy about your age. . . . Whenever he had a minute to himself, he was always going off into the jungle, following the elephant trails." Then Bernard was silent a moment, apparently devoting his whole attention to the jeep. "Well," he concluded, "the jungle didn't really suit him much better than it did the other."

"Did he get melancholia too?" Remy asked timidly.

"No. Machine-gun bullets. He was murdered by terrorists."

The young man, abashed, said nothing, while Bernard watched him out of the corner of his eye. Suddenly he started and seized his weapon; a wild burst of shouting had sprung up all around them. Bernard, remaining quite calm, brought the jeep to a slow stop. The uproar grew louder, and lights shone between the trees.

"What's that?" Remy shouted, unable to control his nerves.

"Just the Tamils reporting for work. We're here."

And since Remy remained somewhat shamefaced over

his excitement, Bernard became a little friendlier. He clapped Remy on the shoulder and added jokingly, "As long as you hear them shouting like that, Remy, everything's all right. It's the terrorists who don't make a sound."

The roll call over, Bernard drove his young assistant toward the village for what he considered the indispensable lesson in authority. Their task was to apprehend the many malingerers who sneaked home under cover of darkness instead of reporting for work. They pursued a number of fugitive shadows; several names were written in the Tamil quartermaster's greasy notebook as the man followed behind, translating the manager's dissatisfaction into shouts.

Suddenly Bernard stopped; his anger had disappeared. He remembered how, twenty years before, he had not been able to keep from laughing at his sheepdog role. Today he played the part mechanically enough, without smiling at all. It was probably a question of age.

He sighed, shrugged his shoulders to shake off such melancholy thoughts, and leaned against one of the concrete posts that supported the village houses: a double row of wooden cottages roofed with corrugated iron. From where they stood, they could see only the open-air kitchens between the pillars, under the raised floors. This was where most of the village's population lived for the larger part of the day. Now that the men were at work, only old people, children, and a few women lingered about this area, where the dirt and disorder of the Indies triumphed over everything.

"It's discouraging work, trying to civilize them," Bernard murmured. "We build them comfortable houses—just look what they do with them."

He pointed to the nearest kitchen, where a cow and her calf were wallowing among the pots, dirty clothes, and half-naked children on the dung-sodden dirt floor. In a sudden fit of rage Bernard began violently abusing the owner, an old man in tatters. A boy untied the cow to lead it away, and the manager pulled his ears to make him move faster. Another name was written in the Tamil's notebook.

The little scene lasted long enough for daylight to transform the plantation: the sun was rising as the two planters, back in the jeep, arrived in the grove of newly tapped rubber trees. Remy was still silent, apparently dreaming.

"Are there attacks very often?" he finally asked.

"You're still worrying about that? I warn you, you'd better start thinking about something else. If you're afraid . . ."

Remy declared he was not thinking of himself but of the dangerous situation of the planters' wives, living in those isolated bungalows. Yesterday, Robert Jourdain's wife had told him she lived in constant fear.

"Helene is too excitable," Bernard grumbled.

"Isn't your wife afraid?"

"Patricia? Afraid?" Bernard's eyes widened as if the question were preposterous.

"I understand," Remy murmured, once again abashed by the manager's attitude. "Your bungalow is protected by the Malay police."

Bernard smiled derisively. "The *mata-matas*? If they

were all we could rely on. . . . Actually, I think it's Pat who protects *them*!"

Bernard stopped the jeep, took off his coat, and got out, dressed now in the planter's typical white uniform: shorts, short-sleeved shirt, knee socks. He was not a talkative man. Nevertheless, while Remy was wondering whether to ask another question, he continued of his own accord, resting one hand on the younger man's shoulder.

"Get this through your head, Remy. Everyone is afraid of something at Kebun Besar. The Tamils are afraid of the European overseers. The Chinese millworkers are afraid of the contractor. The contractor is afraid of the terrorists, who are fleecing him. My assistants are afraid of me. And I'm afraid of the inspections, the letters from the board. . . . But there's one person on the plantation who is an exception to this rule—one person who's not afraid of anyone, Remy," he insisted, his hand pressing harder now, "—not even of me, not even of the board of directors. . . . That person is my wife, young man, my wife Pat."

He spoke with an emphasis that contrasted strongly with his earlier dryness. It was obvious that mention of his wife stimulated him to a passion that the routine work of the plantation could no longer produce. Yet there were certain nuances in his tone Remy was not sure he understood. He glanced sidewise at Bernard, murmuring politely, "A remarkable woman . . . I could tell that as soon as I saw her."

Bernard's hand, which had released his shoulder, tightened a little. He hesitated, searching for the right words to express a complex judgment. At last he said, simply enough, in a toneless voice, as if this were the definitive explanation: "She's an American, Remy."

He remained silent for a moment, apparently considering his own words, then suddenly raised his hand and looked about him. The interval of meditation he occasionally permitted himself was at an end. He resumed his authoritative tone to castigate a Tamil worker who was tapping a rubber tree clumsily.

2　　　　　In her bungalow garden, which covered the rounded top of one of the highest hills of the plantation, Patricia Delavigne was pruning her bougainvillaeas. The sun was not yet very high in the sky, but she had already been up a long time. Patricia was always up early—shortly after Bernard. She regarded idling in bed as a form of moral negligence: it caused her guilt feelings. Besides, all the medical handbooks she consulted advised against it. She had worked out her own regimen, combining the advice of specialists with a dash of her own imagination. She began her day either with a long walk in the rubber groves or a half-hour of calisthenics. After that she worked in her garden, a task that kept her nerves steady and her mind calm without impeding her thoughts, and helped insure a normal metabolism. Afterwards, if she weren't going to Singapore, her time was divided among various chores or spent in reading—for the most part books of an instructive and moralistic nature.

This schedule worked well for her: at forty-four, Patricia looked scarcely thirty-five, despite several years of life below the equator. She was proud of her figure. When she played tennis her legs provoked the other white women of the district—most of them younger than she—to outright jealousy. A less austere discipline had made them vulnerable to the insidious onset of cellulitis.

Her moral health was no less apparent than her physical equilibrium. Primarily it was the product of a warm, generous nature instinctively inclined to consider only the noble aspect of human actions, even if—as Rawlinson often remarked—she had to look rather far and hard to find it; even if she had to expend a considerable amount of energy to isolate and develop it. Such health was sustained by the systematic practice of charity and by daily assistance—in both material and spiritual form—accorded the beings around her who were physically and morally less fortunate than she.

This morning she was wearing dungarees. Usually she wore only shorts and a halter for her domestic tasks. But one day she noticed that the coolies near the bungalow had stopped working and were crouched in the grass nearby, gleefully spying on her every movement. It was on such occasions that Patricia's soul revealed itself in all its greatness. Any other planter's wife would have considered herself offended, would have screamed, called her husband, and been satisfied only after she had seen the transgressors soundly thrashed. But Patricia had merely shrugged her shoulders indulgently. Despising sin, she felt only pity for the culprits and knew how to consider with complete objectivity the sexual problems by which she was not in the least troubled. So she had simply called her houseboy, a faithful French-speaking Chinese who had formerly worked for the steamship lines, and asked him to send the coolies to her. She had lined them up and, with the houseboy as interpreter, improvised in their behalf a sermon on the dangers and degradations of concupiscence. Afterwards she sent them away, dismissing the incident from her mind. It was only to spare her fellow men further temptations that she had subsequently worn more discreet attire.

At the moment she was bending over her bougainvillaeas, she was also being spied on from a distance by the Chinese houseboy and one of the policemen protecting the bungalow; but the sentiments her presence produced in these men were peaceable ones, and quite innocent as well.

The old houseboy was brandishing a feather duster that brushed as silently as a shadow over the living-room furniture. He often interrupted his work to look at the *mem* out of the big bay window and thank heaven he was in her employ. The *Tuan* had his nerves, like all the whites, but the *mem* was the perfect mistress. She had cared for the houseboy with her own hands when he had caught a fever—Patricia had studied medicine a little and worked as a nurse for several years before marrying Bernard—and he was infinitely grateful. She was even an ally sometimes, and since the *Tuan*, despite his severe look, always ended by agreeing to whatever she wanted, the houseboy knew he was sheltered from the storm as long as he was under her protection. Of course there was the tedium of her frequent moralizing—Patricia had a burning desire, a real passion to raise the humble to her own level, and neglected no occasion to do so; but he had grown accustomed to simulating attention, and to answering "yes, *mem*" at the right moment with a conviction that satisfied her without costing him much effort. He was devoted body and soul to his mistress, and she was extremely proud of his loyalty, which served as the conclusive argument in her friendly quarrels with Bernard as to how to treat the natives.

The *mata-mata* on sentry duty at the garden gate was also watching Patricia under his impassive-looking lids. He was one of the Malays hastily recruited from the *kampongs* at the beginning of the troubles and detailed to guard the bungalows. The others were off duty, resting near their bamboo cabin. They were not part of the plantation's personnel, being responsible to Rawlinson, the chief of police. Since the latter made inspections only rarely, it was Bernard who kept track of them, and here, too, thanks to Patricia, the reports were almost always favorable. Patricia felt that they deserved her praise when they brought her some rare flower from the jungle, and she always found excuses for them when they abandoned their post without authorization, which happened frequently. They therefore followed one implicit rule: first of all, satisfy the *mem's* every wish. At this moment the sentry was thinking that it would be pleasant to be dozing over his rifle without having to pretend to be on the lookout, and that the spectacle of a white woman wearing a big hat and men's clothes was interesting to watch.

She stood up, her hands on her hips, to examine the work she had just finished. At first her expression showed satisfaction, but then she frowned. The house-boy and the sentry grew concerned. Her attitude betrayed the fact that the *mem* was annoyed, and the *mem's* annoyance might disturb the bungalow's peace. . . .

"Silly thing," Patricia murmured in English between her teeth, staring at the edge of the lawn with a woebegone look. The lawn was separated from the plantation by a thin strip of wild growth, the last vestige of the jungle that once had covered these hills. A few giant trees remained as well, forming with the underbrush a curtain masking the rubber trees above which only the distant mountains were visible. Since the beginning of the troubles, Bernard had been tempted several times to cut down this thicket that might facilitate the attackers' approach, but Patricia had firmly opposed his resolution. After many discussions and entreaties, he had given his consent only on condition that the whole garden be enclosed with barbed wire, promising that this defense would be quite invisible. The *mata-matas* had set up the fence the day before, while he was away.

"Silly thing," Patricia repeated. Her solitary reflections were usually made in English, although she always spoke French with Bernard, proud of making almost no mistakes.

Far from being invisible, the barbed wire introduced into the garden a certain grim note that she had just discovered. Furthermore, for a stretch of several yards the strands were crushing the flowers in their beds.

"Impossible," she decided. "Hey, boy! *Kebun!*"

In her rare moments of impatience, the bungalow's mistress required a number of people in attendance. The houseboy was already at her side, silent, watchful.

Kebun (Malay for gardener) was meant for any of the *mata-matas*. Never having been able to admit to herself that her bungalow was protected by the police, Patricia had found a title more in accord with the manners of these gentle little men who loved flowers and wore their uniforms as if they were a disguise.

The Malay sentry was about to throw down his rifle and rush to his mistress. All the same, since his corporal had already started up at the *mem's* first cry, he regretfully remained under arms, watching the scene's progress with great interest.

"Take away that horror," Patricia said to the corporal. She always spoke French to the natives. Generally her sign language was sufficiently expressive, but on this occasion the corporal, a young man with boyish gestures, assumed a mournful look of complete incomprehension. There was a decided contradiction between the *Tuan's* orders and the *mem's* desires. When the houseboy had translated the order into Malay, the corporal tried to express the agony his divided loyalties occasioned.

"The *Tuan* has ordered . . ." he began timidly.

"The *Tuan?*" Patricia's eyes flashed. In spite of her kindness, she did not like opposition. But a black scorpion the size of a prawn spared the corporal any further exposure to his dilemma by stinging his bare foot. He screamed and began hopping up and down on the other foot, while the houseboy crushed the creature with a stick. Patricia's heart was touched by the spectacle of such suffering. "The poor boy!" she cried. "That could be very serious."

The *mata-mata* corporal, moved to self-pity by this compassion, burst into heart-rending sobs. The Chinese houseboy considered such conduct lacking in dignity. "Bad, *mem*," he said calmly, "but him not die."

"Not die!" Patricia protested, indignant at such complacency. "He's suffering! Poor boy—lean on me. Come on. . . . You others, help me! He can't even walk."

Her ardor in the unfortunate man's behalf was contagious. The *mata-matas* flew to her assistance, the sentry first of all, after having thrown down his gun. Together they pushed, dragged, and carried the afflicted man toward the bungalow while its mistress authoritatively directed the maneuver. The houseboy had preceded them with a reproachful expression.

"Put him on the couch," Patricia commanded. "Boy, some hot water and my medicine kit."

"It is here, *mem*," said the boy, setting the requested objects beside her.

Under the eyes of the intimidated but curious Malays, who had retreated into a corner of the living room, Patricia began to treat the victim, scolding him in a motherly tone for his bad habit of walking barefoot. She was about to bandage the wound when she heard the sound of a car. It was Bernard coming home. The houseboy tiptoed off to the pantry, and the Malays, suddenly uneasy, began to edge away as the corporal, feeling somehow to blame, half sat up on the couch. But Patricia pushed him down again and immobilized them all with an imperious gesture.

When she had discovered suffering and undertaken to relieve it, it was not in her nature to let herself be interrupted halfway through by external considerations. She must proceed to the end and reap the rewards that a virtuous impulse necessarily implies. Rawlinson, who was very fond of her but for whom she was sometimes an occasion for wonder, claimed that in a perfect world, without poverty or suffering, only Patricia would be unhappy, discontented at not being able to share the accumulated altruism that swelled her compassionate soul.

3   Eager to see the new recruits learn the ropes as soon as possible, Bernard had given Remy several lessons in authority and discipline. In his opinion the white man's conduct in relation to his labor force was one of the most decisive factors of the planter's success. On the way back to his bungalow, he brought the day's experimental demonstrations to a close with this precept: "Above all, never make friends with the natives. In these troubled times this is more important now than ever before. The only way we can keep the least bit of prestige is to keep our distance."

"Yes, sir," Remy said.

The spectacle they encountered on walking into the living room was scarcely a good illustration of this principle. Patricia was maternally stroking the young Malay's cheek, urging him to drink a stimulant she had prepared for him as he lay on the couch. The others were nervously staring at the tracks their dirty feet had left on the carpet.

As usual, the *mem* arranged everything. Confronted by her ingenuous explanations, Bernard, as usual, ended up by agreeing with her. Nevertheless, the *mata-matas* did not get off without a furious scolding for having deserted their posts, though this did not seem to affect them strongly. Patricia insisted on accompanying the corporal to the door, with many recommendations as to the means of avoiding infection, which she insisted that her husband translate. After considerable resistance, he did so to bring an end to an episode he regarded as ridiculous.

The houseboy served them breakfast, and Remy was asked to stay, since he had not yet organized his household. Bernard, whom the sight of a native sprawling on his couch had deeply irritated, could not help reproaching his wife for her excessive sensibility. She took advantage of the situation to explain her point of view once again, and, each in turn calling the young man to witness, husband and wife soon found themselves discussing the terrorists. When Patricia objected to the barbed wire, Bernard wearily began his sermon once again: "Darling, you really are forgetting that these are critical times; our bungalow has already been a target on several occasions; the *mata-matas* are soldiers, they are not here just to obey your whims." It was the voice of reason speaking; Patricia pouted and did not reply.

"Your bungalow has been a target?" Remy asked, exaggerating his curiosity to conceal his embarrassment.

"On an average of one night a month."

"You get used to it very quickly," Patricia broke in. "You'll see, Monsieur Remy."

"And what do you do?"

"What do I do?"

Bernard hesitated for a moment, as if this question had never occurred to him.

"What do I do? I get up . . . Patricia doesn't even get up. I fire the machine gun into the darkness for a little . . . up in the air so as not to hit the sentries . . . to show them I'm here."

There was a touch of embarrassment in his voice, as if he were conscious of the absurdity of these actions even as he was describing them.

"The *mata-matas* barricade themselves in their cabin. They fire up in the air, too. . . . To show me they're there," he added after another moment's thought.

"And the terrorists?"

"They shoot from the next hill, by guesswork. We answer. It's like a game. Little by little things quiet down, and I go to bed."

"Why do they do it?"

"To test our morale, I suppose," Bernard said, suddenly impatient. "Because they are terrorists. To show me they're there, too."

"The terrorists," Patricia said, "are much less dangerous than most people think."

Remarks of this kind, when they did not infuriate Bernard, generally calmed his nerves. He looked at his wife almost tenderly, a little like a wondering animal, and shook his head. "Pat's mission in life, Remy, is to find excuses for the world's worst scoundrels."

Patricia protested that the terrorists were not necessarily scoundrels and, again calling Remy to witness, declared that the English had used the wrong methods with them in this country. "If only they had left things up to you, darling!" Bernard murmured.

With all her authority reawakened, Patricia declared that if things had been left up to her they would have gone much better. And she cited the example of the houseboy she had dealt with so humanely, whose loyalty was so unquestionable. It was an argument Bernard was quite familiar with, and he did not reply. From then on Patricia pressed her advantage, declaring that the only effective and honorable way for the advanced nations to deal with the terrorists was to help them out of their poverty and ignorance. All men, including the natives of this country, and the rebels especially, needed understanding, love, and sympathy.

"Love!" Bernard protested, shrugging his shoulders.

"Love!" Patricia answered in a masterful tone. "Nothing in this world can succeed without love."

Remy felt he must approve his hostess' generous words. But Bernard, if he allowed his wife a number of eccentricities, considered such an opinion out of place in his young assistant's mouth. They had all finished breakfast. He stood up and pointed out rather dryly that Remy could fight the bandits with whatever weapon he chose when he was the plantation's manager—sympathy or love, if he liked—but meanwhile, would he please not forget his machine gun and make sure it was in working order.

It was the day for making up the payroll, and Bernard had decided that Remy should accompany him to the district capital to get the money. They would pick up Robert Jourdain on their way: three armed Europeans were none too many to convoy ten thousand dollars along those roads.

They left in the Delavigne's Ford, taking two Malays with them. Bernard, still annoyed by his wife's remarks, automatically cast about for a scapegoat. He found one at the turn in the road, where a Tamil tapper was scratching at a rubber tree without succeeding in broaching it properly. Bernard leaped out of the car, approached the paralyzed creature, and in a terrible voice demanded to be shown his tapping knife. The Tamil held it out to him, trembling in every limb, his expression pitiful.

"I knew it," screamed the manager of Kebun Besar after running his finger over the chisel's edge. "It's dull. You've been using it to chop up your damn peppers again!"

Everything that affected the plantation's yield caused him a kind of personal pain. He docked the Tamil a day's pay. Appeased, he climbed back in the car and they drove on toward Jourdain's bungalow. Remy said nothing. Suddenly Bernard felt the need to justify himself. "All the same, young man, I don't want you to think I'm an ogre. I have the reputation of being a fair master. . . . When you have responsibilities like mine, you'll learn you can't afford to put up with the slightest negligence. . . . And don't forget that payday has been a bad day these last few years for planters here in Malaya."

The young man tried to redeem himself by declaring that the government should take energetic measures to eliminate such threats. Bernard looked at him ironically. They had reached the Jourdains' bungalow, which resembled Bernard's, though it was slightly smaller and with a less elaborate garden. Robert was waiting for them at the gate.

"Listen to him," said Bernard as he stopped the car. "He's advocating energetic measures to get rid of the terrorists."

"He's quite right," said Helene Jourdain, a thin, rather pretty blonde who had just come out of the house.

Robert merely snorted—it sounded like a sneer. Bernard stretched out his arm, indicating the jungle-covered mountains encircling the plantation.

"Look here, Remy. That's where their nests are. Try to find them! Oh, from time to time 'energetic measures' are taken, as you say. A squadron of R.A.F.'s bombards the jungle. Which is like trying to destroy a school of sardines by machine-gunning the Indian Ocean. It's almost as effective as Pat's methods. . . . They're out there, I tell you," he continued in an anxious tone, "a mile away, or fifty miles—it's all the same to us. And I'd like to know what they're up to . . . especially on payday."

4   The terrorist camp was located on a high ridge less than ten miles from Kebun Besar—ten miles of thick jungle; two hours' march for the partisans; an almost impassable barrier for the Europeans.

In the camp, order and discipline ruled. Kim, the leader, saw to that. From time to time he arranged meetings in which the schoolteacher gave lectures on the duties of the soldiers of the Liberation.

This morning Wang, the schoolteacher, was busy with another chore. He was giving the daily lesson in Mandarin Chinese to the whole camp. This lesson was usually given in the afternoon, but Kim had shifted the schedule, foreseeing a possible raid. It would have taken an extremely serious incident to cause the lessons to be cancelled altogether. Instruction in theory and culture was as important a part of the camp's activities as physical training and the carrying out of raids.

The Party's directives were explicit on this point. Therefore, subject to a heavy program of study and a strict schedule, the terrorists had scarcely more time for their own thoughts than Occidental students.

The lesson was given out of doors. (For rainy days, a big barracks had been thrown together and fitted out as a schoolroom according to Kim's directions.) The schoolteacher stood in front of a large blackboard that Kim had managed to get hold of during a raid and which was rated as essential matériel in case the camp was moved. He was writing the characters in chalk and pronouncing them carefully as he pointed to them with a long bamboo wand. The soldiers, crouching in well-ordered rows, repeated them in chorus after him. Only a few had notebooks and pencils (a special reward for meritorious action) and attempted to form the characters for themselves. Kim was in the first row, and his voice dominated the choir. He outstripped his men in everything—in cold determination, bravery, pitiless cruelty in the hour of battle, as well as in the laborious daily studies.

He looked away from the blackboard for a moment and watched Ling, at his side. She was the only girl in camp and already, despite her years—she was nineteen—one of the best soldiers he had. Although he showed her no partiality, she had recently earned the right to a notebook and a pencil, both by her exemplary conduct and her courage under fire. She was busy copying a character, but her application to this task did not prevent her from repeating the lesson with the others. Kim felt a sudden burst of affection for her, and, lost in a kind of ecstasy, let two characters pass him by.

Usually he did not permit himself to look at Ling

during the lessons. He scarcely spoke to her save to give her orders. In fact, when she had first come, he forbade himself to speak to her alone when he was off duty, as he spoke with the other new recruits to encourage them in the rough and dangerous life they had chosen. The Party was in favor of intimate contact, but with Ling he had kept his distance.

Nevertheless, for several days now his attitude had been changing, and last night, after the self-criticism session that brought the daily lessons to a close, they had exchanged binding vows in the shadow of a great tree. He had nothing to regret. He had recently received a directive that left him in no doubt on the subject: the Party did not forbid love. In fact, it authorized, even recommended, unions among the comrades in camp, provided they were normal, inspired by lasting feelings, and presented no obstacle to service. Kim expected to take advantage of the next important leader's visit to ask him to approve their marriage.

He was still staring at Ling, enraptured by what he saw. He trembled at the thought that last night he had raised his courage to the point of squeezing her hand and caressing her hair. She had not seemed annoyed at his boldness, this little girl who knew better than anyone how to answer Wang's difficult questions, who could throw a grenade farther than most men, and who always aimed carefully before firing, never wasting ammunition.

She noticed that Kim was looking at her, turned her head, and smiled faintly. He felt his heart melt within him and let several more characters pass without speaking. When he recovered, he blamed himself for a serious oversight. He was wondering whether he ought to admit this during the self-criticism session when Sen, his second in command, emerged from the jungle after giving the password to the sentry.

The distracted partisans turned their heads toward him; they knew what his return could mean. The teacher stood abashed before them for a moment, his pointer motionless. Kim gave a sharp order, and the lesson continued. He stood up and went to meet Sen.

"The payroll comes today, comrade," Sen said. "The white devil telephoned the bank yesterday."

"What time?"

"Three o'clock in front of the main office."

There was just time enough to get ready. Kim gave the orders, and the lesson was stopped. The men chosen for the raid ran to get their weapons and show them to their leader, as the rules commanded. In less than two minutes they were lined up, elbow to elbow. Only a few had modern machine guns; the rest had old-fashioned rifles; some, merely pistols.

Ling was second in line, and her skill entitled her to a machine gun. Although he was distressed to have her take part in this expedition, Kim did not feel he had the right to forbid it. He examined the weapon she presented with scrupulous care and could not forbear complimenting her on its perfect condition. Ling was a model soldier.

"Very good, comrade. Go help Sen distribute the ammunition."

It was an honor she deserved. The Party recommended that the leaders reward the best soldiers by such small distinctions. Ling left the row, crimson with pride, and joined Sen in front of a crate near the barracks. Kim continued his inspection.

He was almost finished and had found scarcely any comment to make on the condition of the weapons. The men knew the value of their guns.

But Lao, the last soldier in line, provided him an opportunity to manifest his authority. His rifle showed a number of rust spots. Kim burst into a wild fury on discovering this negligence. Everything that affected his unit's effectiveness, especially the mishandling of precious weapons, drove him beside himself with rage. He shamed Lao publicly for his negligence, in the strongest possible terms. "Show me your knife," he said suddenly.

The unfortunate Lao held it out to him, trembling in every limb, his expression pitiful to see. Kim ran his finger over the blade, and his frown deepened several degrees. He removed Lao from the commando group and summoned Wang, the schoolteacher, who was in charge of all disciplinary matters.

"Dock him a day's pay. His knife is dull. That's the hundredth time I've forbidden it, and he's done it again. He uses it to chop up his damn peppers!"

5   A burning sun overpowered the bungalow, making the flower beds blaze. The *mata-matas*,
sprawling under the trees, their equipment hanging on
the low branches, were resting from their morning's
work: Patricia had made them remove the section of
the barbed-wire fence that spoiled the view and crushed
the flowers. The sentry was asleep on his feet, leaning
against a rubber tree.

Patricia was lying on a chaise longue near the living-
room bay window. She never took a nap, merely relaxed
for an hour after dinner. She had eaten quite late, alone,
for Bernard would not be home until evening, after the
payroll had been made up. She forced herself to think
of nothing in order to relax completely.

She had almost succeeded when a burst of machine-
gun fire echoed in the distance. She lay quite still for a
second, astonished. A louder fusillade exploded. It was

something serious. She rushed into the garden, where she found the houseboy, trembling, listening warily. In front of their cabin the *mata-matas,* after the first moment of surprise, were quickly buckling on their equipment. Patricia listened anxiously. There were several more bursts of fire, then a few isolated shots and a muffled explosion that was probably a grenade.

"Lord! That's coming from the main office!"

"The payroll, *mem,*" the houseboy said, frowning. "Very bad."

He ran into the bungalow and began to close all the windows. When he was finished he came out on the veranda again and pleaded with his mistress: "Inside, *mem.* The *Tuan* has ordered. Not to leave the bungalow when there are shootings."

"Leave me alone," Patricia said. Once her first excitement had passed, she felt all her indomitable energy revive within her. . . . The police must be informed.

She walked into the living room and picked up the telephone.

"No good, *mem.* Already tried. Telephone cut."

She threw down the receiver furiously, walked outside again, and hurried toward the *mata-matas,* who were in complete disorder. The corporal, his foot bandaged, seemed unable to decide what to do. She berated him. "You must all go in the jeep. All of you, bring help."

The houseboy translated. The corporal protested timidly. "The *Tuan* has said, 'In case of alarm, not to move, to protect the *mem.*'"

"The *mem* . . . the *mem* can take care of herself! They're not after me. Tell them, boy; if they refuse, I'll go myself, and get them all fired."

Confronted with this threat, the Malays no longer hesitated. They piled into the jeep and disappeared in the direction of the office. Patricia remained alone with the houseboy, who trembled at each new round of shots.

She waited for more than an hour, her anxiety growing every second, reproaching herself for not having gone with the police. There had been no firing for a long time. Sometimes she thought she could hear something in the direction of the office, but it was only her imagination. The rubber-tree forest muffled every sound.

Reluctantly, the houseboy offered to take his old bicycle to find out what was happening. She was about to accept when the telephone bell made her start. It was Bernard. Communications had just been re-established. He was calling to tell her he was all right. Patricia sighed; she loved him dearly.

"Everything's all right, darling," he said quickly. "It's all over. They missed their chance, but we were lucky . . . only one guard slightly wounded. That's all."

"I'm so glad you're all right, dear!" Patricia said. "And what about them?"

Bernard's voice echoed the emotions of the battle. "We saw one of them go down. Remy and Robert are out on patrol now—he won't get away. I'm waiting for Rawlinson with the dogs. If they find him . . ."

Her anxiety calmed, Patricia could not help urging moderation. Bernard's tone of voice betrayed his impatience. "Oh, Pat darling, I tell you this is no time to preach Christian charity to me . . . I'll see you tonight."

She walked slowly out into the garden, reflecting. The sun was beginning to set. Not the least wind stirred in the great jungle trees around the bungalow. She suddenly felt alone and sad. The houseboy timidly approached and asked, "The *Tuan* not wounded?"

"No," Patricia answered absent-mindedly.

"Many terrorists killed?"

The question had a greedy accent that made her lift her head and scowl.

"I hope not," she said severely. "Don't talk about it any longer—go make me some tea."

The houseboy went off to the kitchen, crestfallen. Patricia felt her solitude all the more acutely. She wanted to tell someone how she felt. After a moment's hesitation she decided to call Helene Jourdain.

Helene, too, had heard the sound of shooting and was still trembling from her scare. Robert had just called to reassure her. Patricia could not get in a word. For more than ten minutes Helene drowned her with complaints about her terrible plight, and ended by saying she hoped the wounded man would be made to pay for the others who had escaped. She had seen Rawlinson's car from her bungalow, which was near the main road. Now she could hear the hounds, and a sort of jubilation filled her voice as she described the manhunt getting under way.

"Hysteria," Patricia wailed as she hung up sadly.

She sighed and told herself she had made a mistake looking for understanding from that brainless little egotist. Even Bernard, though he loved her, understood her so little.

She went out into the garden, where the houseboy brought the tea. The low sun was tolerable now. She sat there for more than a quarter of an hour, managing little by little to recover her serenity in the awareness of her moral superiority, when a sudden noise made her lift her head. It seemed to come from the narrow strip of jungle separating the bungalow from the plantation. Patricia listened attentively.

6　　　　To be taken alive by the white devils was the terrible nightmare that had obsessed Ling's feverish mind ever since she had collapsed with a bullet in her leg, for she entertained no illusions about her fate. Nevertheless, it was not the sensation of the rope around her neck that made her tremble, or the awareness of the physical sufferings that would precede her execution; it was the vision of a circle of whites leaning over her, alternating promises and threats, grinning at her defeat and touching her with their pale hands.

Ling hated the whites. In Singapore, where she had grown up, her mother had augmented her wretched shopkeeper's income by selling herself to them. She was only an amateur prostitute. Occasionally two or three rickshaw drivers she gave tips to brought her a customer—a tourist, a planter who had no time to waste, a businessman who considered himself too high on the social ladder to risk a visit to professionals. For Ling and her sisters these visits meant a sudden awakening and orders to sleep in a shed behind the house. She had therefore learned to consider the whites as intruders long before she learned what they came for. The day she understood, she could not stand the house another moment and ran away to the terrorists. She had found in their ranks several bloody opportunities to appease her resentment, and the camp's monastic life satisfied her fierce longing for purity.

Now all that remained of her strength and energy was in the service of a single goal: not to be taken alive. She must drag herself into the jungle, a natural shelter against the greatest dangers. The force of her will had helped her overcome the pain and think clearly when she had fallen near the main office at the edge of the irrigation ditch. She could expect no help. The attack had been a failure. In spite of the danger of her situation, she still felt the bitterness of failure, knowing how necessary the payroll money was to the life of the camp and her comrades. A clumsy partisan had knocked his rifle against a rock as he was crawling toward the point from which the attack was to be launched. One of the whites had raised his head; she had seen him quite distinctly from the bush where she had taken cover. It was the oldest of the three, the one who looked as if he were the leader. Then the same partisan had lost his nerve. He was a novice; he thought he had been discovered and began firing wildly. The white had not taken long to shoot back.

And the first bullet had been for her, although in all fairness it was the clumsy comrade whom heaven ought to have punished! But this was no time for finding fault. After the first shock of pain, Ling had looked at her leg:

it was bleeding. The comrades had turned back under Kim's orders, firing through the trees. Kim had not seen her fall. She had not cried out, for she must not distract the leader from his work. She could count only on herself.

So she painfully dragged herself as far as the ditch and rolled in. Now her blood would leave no tracks behind her. Even dogs could not follow her trail. The water was shallow, but the strong current carried her across the weeds; she clenched her teeth when her wounded leg scraped the bottom.

The ditch made several turns, crossing a series of gullies. Over her head passed the hills planted with rubber trees. She did not know where she was being carried, but what was most important was to get away from the office. Her mind did not stop working, in spite of the pain. She was afraid her stratagem would not hold off the police for long; they would certainly think of following her downstream. And then . . . again she shuddered at the thought. High above her Ling noticed a group of trees. She felt dizzy. Like an exhausted pilgrim who, after losing all hope of reaching his goal, sees the temple of his faith rising out of the clot of miserable huts ahead of him, Ling discovered the giant trees rising toward the sky above the forest of rubber trees.

The jungle! She knew the plantation's boundaries extended beyond the hilltops. These trees, she recognized, could not be a hallucination; she felt quite clearheaded, despite her weakness. Freedom lay in this direction.

After a thousand efforts that cost her ever-increasing pain, she managed to get out of the irrigation ditch. She stopped a second, anxiously measuring the ground to be covered. She would have to have strength enough to get up that hill—then she would be safe. Before starting to crawl up the slope she tore off the cuff of her trouser leg and tied a plaster of mud and leaves over the wound to keep it from bleeding.

It took her more than an hour to get to the top. By the time she reached it, she was exhausted, but she felt she must penetrate farther into the jungle before resting. She reached the shadow of the tall trees at the cost of a last effort, dragged herself a little farther, and then her strength failed her. She groaned, and fainted.

Patricia heard the groan at the same moment she made out a human shape at the edge of the garden. The houseboy had heard it too. He stood perfectly still for a moment, his neck stiffened, head stretched toward this unaccustomed presence that, in the night's silence, assumed the shape of a terrible threat. Ling made a last movement before losing consciousness, and the Chinese recognized the red-starred cap she had firmly pulled down on her head in order to leave no clues behind her.

"Not to go near, *mem!*" he cried. "Very bad. Terrorist."

But this warning could not prevent Patricia from bringing succor to someone in pain. She rushed through the gap in the barbed wire, reached the bushes, discovered Ling prostrate before her, and stood astonished.

"A *girl!*" she murmured. "Poor little thing!"

The houseboy, who had rushed back into the bungalow, now cautiously approached, armed with a long kitchen knife. He found his mistress on her knees, her ear pressed against Ling's chest, her expression anxious.

At this moment the baying of dogs broke out in the distance. Patricia lifted her head, her face set, and saw the houseboy brandishing his weapon.

"Throw that away!"

He obeyed reluctantly. More howling could be heard now. Patricia thought rapidly. "She can't be left here," she said finally, and her voice was firm. "Help me carry her."

"Where, *mem?*"

"Into the bungalow . . . into the guest room; no one ever goes in there. They won't look for her there."

"We party to crime, *mem,*" the houseboy said, hesitating. He looked down, for he did not like the way his mistress stared at him.

"Listen to me," Patricia said, a sudden calmness in her manner. "If the police find her here, they will kill her right away or else hang her later, won't they?"

"Yes, *mem.*"

"Then we would be party to a much worse crime. Have you forgotten what I taught you? You must forgive your enemies. You must love them."

"Yes, *mem,*" the boy said again without conviction.

"Well, pick her up. What are you waiting for?"

"All right, *mem,*" the boy said obediently. She helped him lift Ling onto his shoulder and carry her to the bungalow. The machine gun, which the girl had dragged up the slope with her, lay next to the cap. Patricia picked them both up, tossing her head. The baying seemed closer. She shrugged her shoulders, looked carefully around her, and removed all traces of the girl.

When Rawlinson, accompanied by a band of policemen, reached the bungalow after having followed almost all of Ling's itinerary, he found Patricia calmly finishing her tea. Night was falling, but the veranda lamp illuminated the garden. The Englishman and his men crossed the screen of jungle growth by the light of their flashlights. Patricia gasped as she noticed the silhouettes of two enormous dogs running through the bushes.

"Hello, John!" she cried, walking to meet him. "I'm half dead with worry. Bernard wasn't hurt, was he?"

"Not one bit, Pat. He just stayed behind at the office to finish the payroll and put things in order. He'll be back late. And I'm simply out of my mind—we've lost that bandit's tracks."

"Really?"

The policeman looked around him. "He probably jumped into the irrigation ditch . . . that's what I would have done in his place. The current must have carried him pretty far. They'll find his body one of these days. . . . Unless. . . . The dogs seem to have found something near the bungalow." He fell silent and looked at her questioningly.

"Whisky, John?" Patricia asked. "Boy!"

"Here, *mem,*" the houseboy said, bringing out the tray.

"The dogs . . ." Rawlinson repeated in a preoccupied tone, mechanically picking up the glass. "You didn't hear anything, Pat?"

"Not a thing. I haven't left the garden since the first alarm. Your dogs must have smelled my tracks. I always walk down to the ditch. I was there this morning."

Rawlinson said nothing, watching the houseboy. "Are you sure of this boy?" She assumed a look of wounded dignity and declared that she would answer for the boy's loyalty as for her own. Rawlinson murmured an absent-minded "Ahhh!" He could not help thinking there were some strange aspects to this business. The dogs had headed straight toward the bungalow. And this boy? He knew these Chinese. He could have sworn this boy's face was trying to cover up for something as he avoided his look, much too absorbed in the tray. The police officer stared at Patricia, shrank from her candid gaze, and turned away his eyes. The suspicion that had occurred to him for an instant was ridiculous. He knew her generosity, of course. In spite of the ironic reflections she sometimes drove him to, he felt something like tenderness for her. She was capable of a lot of nonsense, but it was impossible to suspect her in a case like this.

All the same, he went through the forms of asking her if he could glance at the kitchen and the boy's room, to which she agreed with a shrug of her shoulders.

He returned after a moment, crestfallen. She asked him jokingly if he wanted to search her own bedroom, or the whole bungalow. He looked at her one last time, hesitated, and then decided to laugh it off, confessing that he had drawn a blank. He and his men left soon after, with many excuses, in a truck that had come to meet them. Patricia watched them fade into the dark underbrush, where the fireflies traced their tiny signals in the dusk.

"Boy, you boil some water and bring me my kit."
"All ready, *mem,*" the boy said.
"And a pair of pajamas. She can't be left like this."
Patricia leaned over Ling's body and examined her

wound. While she was in this position the Chinese girl opened her eyes. When the houseboy returned, he found Ling with a dagger in her hand about to stab his mistress. He threw himself upon her and twisted her arm. She fell back with a scream of pain. Patricia straightened up.

"Be careful!" she said, outraged at the boy's violence. "What a way to treat an invalid. . . . Poor darling," she continued, caressing Ling's hair. "How you must have suffered! I'm your friend; I don't want to hurt you. Boy, tell her that."

Reluctantly the houseboy translated her words. Ling, who had shrunk beneath Patricia's hand, remained silent, her eyes wide with fury and scorn.

"Tell her the police have gone."

The boy explained the situation ill-naturedly. Ling answered in a few harsh syllables.

"What is she saying?" Patricia asked, beginning to wash the wound, paying no further attention to the dagger Ling was still holding.

"She say, 'The *Tuan* will give her to police.' "

Patricia straightened up, indignant. "Never. The *Tuan* will do as I say. Tell her that," she continued vehemently, giving the boy a push. "You can see she's dead with fear. Tell her the *Tuan* always does as I wish. . . . Go on, explain it to her, explain to her that I'm an American!"

The boy obeyed. Ling let herself be cared for without protesting as Patricia deployed her skills in silence. She discovered that the bullet had passed through the leg without causing any serious damage and she was sure enough of herself to know she could clear up the wound without calling in a doctor. That was all that mattered. She dressed the wound, gave the girl an injection while the latter watched her defiantly, her teeth clenched. When she was through she stood up, contemplated her patient with a smile, and held out her hand. "Will you give me that?"

Ling hesitated for a second, then handed over the dagger. "It's all in the way you do it," Patricia murmured triumphantly. She gave the boy the weapons and the cap and ordered him to bury them all in the garden; then she turned back toward the Chinese girl and with motherly gestures began to take off the dirty clothes and help her into her own pajamas.

7　　　　It was only three days later, on Sunday, that Patricia decided to reveal to her husband the presence of an unsuspected guest in their bungalow. She could not wait any longer. At any moment Bernard might go into the back bedroom where she was caring for Ling in secret, with the houseboy's reluctant complicity. On the other hand, she had calculated that this delay would now confront him with a *fait accompli*.

She knew he would be furious and that despite her power over him it would be difficult to prevail in this matter. After having carefully recapitulated her various arguments while he was still napping, she went into Ling's room, bathed her, and after several entreaties that the boy translated, persuaded the Chinese girl to let her arrange her hair and lightly make up her face.

"The *Tuan* is coming to see you. . . . Oh, don't be

afraid, he'll do as I say; but it will make things so much easier if you're a little more presentable!"

A little later she joined her husband, who had been napping in a dressing gown on the veranda. He was staring hard at the gap in the barbed wire and seemed preoccupied. He made some remark about the wounded terrorist and expressed regret that he had been able to escape. It was her opportunity, and she took it.

"I know how he escaped," she said casually.

"What?"

"I said I know how he escaped," she said very calmly. "And I know where he is hiding."

While her astonished husband stared at her in silence, she continued. "He's here, darling. . . . Oh, don't be angry. You'll see why I couldn't do anything else. First of all, it's not a he, it's a *she*."

"*She!*"

Patricia took advantage of his confusion to tell how she had found Ling; the girl was almost a child: the most elementary notion of humanity had kept her from letting the girl be devoured by the dogs.

"And you're saying she's . . . here?"

"Right here, dear, in the guest room."

"The *guest* room!" Bernard suddenly shouted, his anger exploding at the word's extravagance.

"Please don't shout!"

With an anxious look toward the bungalow, she quickly put her hand over his mouth, and in the tone of an attentive nurse that enraged him still more, said, "The fever has fallen some, but she needs care and absolute calm . . . as well as a lot of affection. Think of what she's been through!"

"Affection!"

Each of her fantastic words emphasized the melodramatic character of the situation his wife had put him in. Accustomed as he was to her eccentricities, it still took him quite a while to recover his equanimity. When he finally succeeded in becoming somewhat calmer he reproached her bitterly for her foolishness, attempting to point out the dangers she had brought down on his head as well as on her own, for he would be suspected of being her accomplice.

Patricia listened to him without objections, her expression as obedient and contrite as a child who knows he has misbehaved. She interrupted him only when he told her it was not at all impossible she could be hung for what she had done: the English did not consider such actions a joking matter.

"Oh dear," she cried earnestly, "they wouldn't dare hang me. I've kept my American citizenship."

Such ingenuousness, such sovereign naïveté would have disarmed him now as it had so many times before, had this been a trifle that was in question. But the situation was really serious. "Three days!" he cried despairingly. "How can we get the police to believe we didn't know she was here!"

When Patricia, with a look of pleased conviction, agreed that it was absolutely impossible, Bernard had another fit of rage on discovering the houseboy was in the secret, too. Recognizing the futility of discussion, he tried to control himself and find a way out of their difficulties. The prospects of the only solution he could reasonably imagine were not reassuring. He felt trapped. Here he was, the manager of Kebun Besar, obliged to sneak around like a criminal in order to transport the wretched creature as far as possible from the plantation. "And all that," he groaned, "so she can get back to those bandit friends of hers and, thanks to me, thanks to you, continue to steal from us, ruin us, murder us. . . . Oh, Pat, Pat, you've really behaved like a lunatic!"

But Patricia, whom the most violent reproaches left quite unmoved when she had made up her mind, merely pricked up her ears at her husband's decision and immediately made it clear that he must not even dream of putting it into effect. "It's quite impossible, dear," she declared in a categorical tone. "We simply haven't the right to send a child her age back to a life of crime and debauchery among a band of lawless fanatics. It would be a terrible sin."

His voice trembled as he protested that it was scarcely a time to speak of morality, or of sin either. She agreed with him docilely enough, her face thoughtful, and declared, "I have an idea."

This remark merely increased her husband's agitation; now openly distressed, he asked her to explain what she had in mind. First she insisted that he come— on tiptoe, quietly—and see the child. He ended by agreeing, reluctantly enough, grumbling that he knew quite well what such bandits looked like.

They had reached the end of the hallway, in front of the guest-room door. The bungalow was absolutely quiet. At Bernard's first outburst the houseboy had hidden himself in the kitchen, from which he invisibly followed the scene's progress, hoping the *Tuan* would get rid of the intruder.

Patricia put a finger to her lips, opened the door, and flicked on the light. There was Ling, stretched out on her bed, her eyes wide open, her face pale, wearing a pair of pajamas far too big for her. Thanks to Patricia's skill she had lost some of her fierce expression, and, besides, she was a very pretty girl. Disarmed, weakened, she looked quite different from anything Bernard had expected. He stood stock-still for a moment, astonished, almost touched. He was confused, carefully concealed his feelings, and turning toward Patricia asked with a certain severity in his voice, "All right, I've seen her. What's your idea?"

"We must keep her here with us, dear," Patricia murmured in her gentlest manner.

"What!"

Ling shrank back at this exclamation. Patricia quickly closed the door behind them, scolding Bernard as she did so. Then she began to plead her cause, methodically combining entreaty and persuasion with all the authority her ardent feelings inspired. "Now listen to me, Bernard. We have no children. It's Providence that has sent this girl to us. We must not reject her. If she stays with us, her bitter feelings will little by little disappear. We'll teach her the laws and morality of the civilized world; we'll give her a Christian education and know the joy of having saved a soul. It's such a wonderful mission, dear!"

Bewildered and overpowered by such arguments, Bernard was beginning to lose ground. He murmured between his teeth that he didn't give a damn about her soul, but with less conviction than he liked. Patricia pushed open the door again.

"Look at her carefully. You can see that she has a fine nature—it's written all over her face. All she needs is a charitable hand to lead her toward the Good."

Bernard looked at Ling again, for a long time. When he turned back to Patricia, there was a slight overtone of regret in his voice in spite of himself. "You know it's impossible, Pat. How could we account for the sudden appearance of a Chinese girl in our house?"

But she was not to be stopped by such details. They would claim to have found Ling in Singapore, where her family happened to live; it was true anyway—Patricia had found out everything through the houseboy. They would make up some story of missing papers and, once Bernard answered for her, they could easily get her a new card of identity from Rawlinson. She would see to it herself.

It was still a dangerous caprice. He knew it was, and yet his protests grew increasingly weaker. She decided to make him consent without leaving him time to think. In a businesslike tone, as if logic and good sense were all that mattered to her, she summed up the situation: "After all, it's very simple. You said so yourself; we can't hand her over to the police. We would be accused of being accomplices and be sentenced. Isn't that true?"

"Yes, that's right."

"Good. And we can't send her back to that unspeakable life. It would be a terrible responsibility. We could never look each other in the face again. Am I right or wrong?"

"Yes, of course," he answered weakly, overcome by her accent of conviction.

"So, dear, there's only one solution. She *must* stay with us."

"Only one solution," he repeated.

She gave a cry of joy and threw herself into his arms. She had won.

For an instant he had an indefinable hallucination: the sense of being on a steep mountain with a guide who had gone crazy, who was trying to lead him over a precipice by promising him he would be safe there. The strangest thing was that it was not unpleasant, and that his mind gradually let itself approve his guide's dangerous eccentricities. Pat's revelations, the vision of Ling, an indomitable enemy, coddled under his own roof, his wife's preposterous plea in the girl's defense— everything contributed to the overwhelming brew that completely conquered his powers of resistance. His confusion broke out in a flood of disconnected words that betrayed his complete defeat. He cupped Patricia's head between his two hands, while she kept her arms about him, in order to look at her more closely.

"Let her stay with us, darling, let her stay, even if it brings us both to the gallows! Let her stay, let her betray us, let her cut our throats one of these days; I'd prefer anything to going through the hell of another argument with you!"

He broke off to kiss her tenderly, beneath Ling's hostile, scornful gaze, then continued in the same passionate tone. "Darling, darling, you've won. I agree to everything. But please tell me where you get your fantastic sense of logic—where you find these perverse reasons that end up making the wildest follies seem the only sensible thing to do. Explain it to me. . . ." He had to find a rationale in incoherence, even while he felt himself drawn toward it as if it were a vice, a drug. Patricia, who had not realized the desperate character of his protests, smiled at his blindness. She pressed herself a little closer to him and murmured in a tone of gentle reproof, "But, darling, you know—I'm an American."

PART TWO

8   During the month that followed the raid, Bernard's mind was preoccupied by the approach of a major event: the visit of the Company's most important administrator, Count d'Erival, the son of the founder, the great d'Erival whose portrait hung in the managerial offices of every plantation in Malaya. When he had time to think, Bernard realized that this inspection worried him far more than the presence of a terrorist in his bungalow and made the risk of a few years' hard labor seem almost unworthy of consideration.

The afternoon before the great day, he walked into the main office, which was the scene of feverish activity. Two Tamil crews were scrubbing the hallways, and a number of women were cutting the lawn in front of the building with mowers improvised from a kind of revolving scythe. Children were picking up pieces of dead wood and carrying them off to a gully invisible from the road. Some Chinese workmen were painting the front of the building; others were whitewashing the concrete pillars. Several *mata-matas,* whose official duty did not extend beyond protection of the building, had nevertheless joined in the work, caught up in the general air of expectancy. They were weaving palm and fern garlands to be hung along the fence surrounding the lawn.

At the sight of Bernard, the general excitement became more frenzied. Scarcely paying any attention, he got out of the jeep and walked into the clerks' room, a huge hall in which the order and uniformity of big business triumphed over such local disturbances. From one end to the other, identical desks were lined up in rows at equal intervals. At each desk, in front of a typewriter, sat a Tamil or Chinese clerk in long trousers and a white shirt. Against the rear wall a mass of gray filing cabinets formed a new barricade. Framed graphs, charts, and columns of figures representing the financial profits of Kebun Besar were hung round the walls.

Mr. Gopal, the white-haired Tamil head clerk, stood up to greet his superior. "Good afternoon, sir."

Bernard answered absent-mindedly and asked for the hundredth time if everything was in order. Mr. Gopal, his reply betraying no failure of alacrity, answered that he believed so. He was an old, loyal employee in whom Bernard had complete confidence. For certain details, however, he relied only on himself.

He walked slowly around the room, followed by Mr. Gopal, while the other clerks bent over their work. He checked the alignment of the desks and the equality of the intervals separating them. Then he stopped and ran his finger along the top of one of the filing cabinets. It had become black with grease, and Bernard's voice rose. "Is this what you call 'in order,' Mr. Gopal?"

It was the sort of detail a subordinate's eye never caught. Filled with confusion, old Gopal stammered his excuses and gave a sharp order. An office boy rushed up, armed with a rag. Bernard continued his rounds and stopped near the door. "Tomorrow morning I want all the clerks here at seven. . . . Make it six-thirty," he amended testily.

"Very well, sir."

"And everyone in white trousers, of course—clean shirts, collars, ties . . . and jackets. I insist on that."

"I'll make a preliminary inspection myself, sir," said Mr. Gopal calmly. Bernard stared at him wonderingly, seemed about to add something, remained silent another minute. Then he turned his eyes toward the teams of men and women working outside the building. He pointed to the *mata-matas* gaily weaving garlands into an arch over the gate.

"What the devil are they doing?"

"To give a cheerful look to the place, sir," said Gopal, hesitating. . . . "It was an idea they had," he added, pointing to the Malays. "I let them go ahead. . . . Don't you approve, sir?"

After his first glance Bernard had felt such decorations were harmless enough, but on reflection he decided they were inadmissible and ordered them removed. "A visit from our chief administrator, Count d'Erival, has nothing to do with a carnival, Mr. Gopal," he said harshly—despite certain appearances to the contrary, he added to himself. "He might think us whimsical inside the offices as well as out . . . and we are not whimsical, are we, Mr. Gopal?" he insisted, watching the man out of the corner of his eye.

"Certainly not, sir," the old clerk replied with a woebegone expression.

Once again Bernard stared insistently at his old employee, as if he were looking for some occult, profound significance in these banal replies. Despairing of finding any, he left, after arranging with Gopal to make a last unhurried check that evening of the administrative and financial situation at Kebun Besar.

Alone in his jeep, Bernard made the circuit he would take tomorrow with the Administrator. All along the route Tamil crews were busy with a general clean-up. He drove as far as the bridge over the canal at the plantation's entrance, where Chinese workmen under Remy's supervision were whitewashing the balustrades. He crossed the bridge, drove on several hundred yards, turned around, and slowly returned, forcing himself to examine everything with the eyes of a stranger from the outside world. He did not find much to say, made a few observations to Remy for form's sake, and drove back to the office. On his way he met Robert Jourdain coming from the mill. "Is everything all right over there?"

Robert replied that he had had a dress rehearsal; the workers' movements were like a ballet. Tomorrow each man would be wearing a new sarong. The aluminum vats were shining like suns. For eight days the whole work force had been busy polishing them.

Their eyes met and the two men burst out laughing. With Robert, a planter almost as experienced as him-

66

self, Bernard could forget his painful obligation to appear severe and did not conceal the annoyance this visit was causing him. They exchanged a few half-joking, half-bitter remarks. "I hope the terrorists won't spoil our charming day for us."

"Don't even mention the terrorists," Bernard said hurriedly. "They've been lying low for over a month."

His face darkened as he climbed back into the jeep to go home for a cup of tea. Robert watched him drive off and shrugged his shoulders. After glancing bleakly at the Malays making off with the last of their triumphal arch, he murmured that he would be delighted not to mention the terrorists. But they existed nevertheless, and, at least, were living in a real world, were they not?

As a matter of fact, a little before sunset, in the terrorist camp deep in the jungle, Kim was walking up and down the schoolroom followed by Wang, the schoolmaster responsible for disciplinary and hygienic matters. It was a long room built, like the other barracks, of bamboo and raw wood, but more carefully, and its arrangement of rustic furniture suggested a meticulous organization.

The schoolmaster's desk was placed at the rear, next to the precious blackboard, on a dais of beaten earth. The middle of the schoolroom was occupied by several rows of parallel benches. On each side, against the walls, separated by regular intervals, were open filing cabinets containing the camp's many documents and accounts, for when the room was not full of men eager for learning, it served as Wang's office on the occasions when he doubled as the camp's executive secretary. For this additional service he required two assistants—two soldiers whom Kim had detailed from commando duty to complete his administrative staff, and who were extremely proud of their promotion. Both were there now, bent over their lists of figures, while Kim was making his tour of inspection.

Kim seemed disturbed. He checked the alignment of the filing cabinets, then took a thread out of his pocket and measured the intervals that separated them. He looked reassured. But suddenly he walked toward the blackboard, thrust a finger into a corner, and examined it: it was white with chalk dust. "You call that 'in order'?" he snapped.

Wang blushed with shame and barked a harsh order. A sentry on duty at the door rushed up, rag in hand. Kim felt a pang of conscience at this negligence. He had to look after the slightest details himself; Wang was conscientious enough but did not understand the importance of Comrade Ho's tour of inspection tomorrow. Comrade Ho was one of the most important leaders of the terrorist general staff, a man who was in contact with the People's Republic of China, who had shaken the hand of Mao Tse-tung. Kim made several more suggestions and left the schoolroom.

In spite of the lateness of the hour, there was still a good deal of feverish—if well-organized—activity around the barracks. Kim sighed, thinking how his carefully worked-out schedule had been completely disorganized for the last eight days by the approaching inspection. Divided into several specialized teams—weeding, cleaning, painting, miscellaneous carpentry—the partisans had neglected their usual chores in order to devote themselves to the embellishment of the unit. Kim himself had given orders to this effect. He knew all too well the importance great leaders attached to appearances.

He walked gravely down the path lined with gray stones leading to the schoolroom. Some soldiers were whitewashing the stones. At the end of the path he turned around, trying to imagine Comrade Ho's first impression on his arrival. He was distracted from this effort by Sen, who had come to assure him that everything was ready.

"Tomorrow," Kim said, "I want the uniforms to be perfect—not one tear, not one spot."

"Yes, Comrade," Sen said. "I won't be here, as you know, but Wang will conduct an early-morning inspection." They continued their rounds, stopping at the camp gate. Two partisans were erecting a triumphal arch made of flowers and shrubs they had gathered in the jungle.

"What's that?" Kim asked roughly.

Sen looked worried, and hesitated before replying: "It's Comrade Chao's idea"—pointing to the younger of the two partisans, who could scarcely have been more than sixteen—"he thought it would honor our great leader Ho. It seemed a good idea, so I let him go ahead. . . . Don't you agree, Comrade?"

Kim seemed to be struggling with contradictory feelings. He thought for a moment before reaching a decision. "Our leader Ho," he said at last, "is coming here to inspect our work. He must be received with order, of course—that is the only way good work can be done—but without luxury. That decoration is a sign of frivolity."

"Yes, Comrade," Sen said.

He gave the crestfallen Chao orders to take down the structure.

"That wasn't a good idea," Sen added to Chao. "Don't forget to mention it in the self-criticism session. I'm making a note of it for myself, too, since I told you it was all right."

Kim watched the young man, who lowered his eyes.

"You might explain that you meant well," Kim said. "I suppose you did."

"Oh yes, Comrade," said Chao, his eyes shining.

"That's an explanation, not an excuse. . . . Oh, Sen, Sen," Kim continued as they walked away, his voice betraying a sudden despair, "we have no cause to be raising triumphal arches. And we certainly have no right to be patting ourselves on the back! We're so negligent—we're not even good soldiers. I blame myself first of all. That raid we bungled last month at Kebun Besar was all my fault. I must have prepared it badly."

Sen replied bitterly that it was everyone's fault. They had not been fast enough. But Kim could not forgive himself. The mention of their failure and its consequences reopened the wound in his heart. "Ling," he murmured, "Ling, our best soldier. Lost—lost, and all my fault."

"She may not be dead. The spies have not yet been able to find her."

"Then it's all the worse. Her martyrdom will only last longer." Kim closed his eyes, overcome by weakness. He had to summon up all his pride of leadership to surmount the hideous vision that had been dancing before his eyes this past month. Ling in a dungeon, Ling dying of hunger, Ling abused, mercilessly beaten by the police before they put the rope around her neck.

9   "Take a little more honey, Ling, dear. It's jungle honey—the Malays brought it for me."

Sitting beside Patricia, Ling looked sourly at the tray covered with sandwiches, cookies, and fruit—a tea that would have constituted a whole dinner for a starving man. Since Patricia had taken the girl under her protection, she had tried every means in her power to tame her, and supposed that the gastronomic refinements of the civilized world might represent a powerfully persuasive factor. But Ling rejected all her advances. She looked at the delicacies with the expression of a tiger offered a bowl of milk. At first she had refused to eat anything at all. For the last few days, however, she had been doing better, for she had decided that she might need all her strength in the near future. But she usually helped herself when her benefactress' back was turned and ate in secret in order not to give her the satisfaction of scoring a point.

She shook her head and snorted.

"You have to eat, Ling!" Patricia insisted. "You're well now, your color is coming back; but you're still much too thin."

She spoke to the girl in French, carefully articulating each word. She had decided to teach her the language, and gave her a lesson every day. Ling was a good student, interested in spite of herself by so many new ideas. She already knew many words, and could guess the meaning of a surprising number of sentences; but here, as well, her pride forced her to conceal at least half of her progress.

"Non'g," she answered, using the word that described her attitude toward all such advances, the word that formed the essential part of her conversation.

"You must say *'Non, merci,'* dear."

"Non'g mer-ci," Ling drawled resentfully.

Patricia did not insist. No rebuff could discourage her or turn her from her purpose. She led the girl into a corner of the living room for the daily lesson. Somewhere she had gotten hold of an illustrated child's reader. From it she would read aloud a sentence, taking care to pronounce correctly, and the Chinese girl would repeat it after her. Ling obeyed, deliberately making mistakes. The houseboy stood at a distance, waiting for his mistress to call upon his services as a translator. Ling never looked at him; she felt a distaste for him even more intense than her hatred of the American woman.

"Boy, tell her that when she can speak nicely, without making mistakes, I'll give her a lovely present."

Ling maintained a stubborn silence. Patricia took up the book again. *"Le tigre est un an-i-mal crou-el . . . crou-el . . ."* she repeated; the sound of the word apparently disconcerted the girl. Suddenly Ling turned her head, having heard Bernard's jeep. "All right now, Ling . . . let's show him the progress you're making: *'le ti-gre . . .'* "

Ling concentrated and spoke the sentence almost perfectly as Bernard appeared on the doorstep. He looked at the two women in silence while the boy hurried off for fresh tea. The sight of his wife giving French lessons to a Chinese terrorist under this Malayan roof calmed his nerves somewhat. He forgot his professional troubles for a moment.

"Don't you think she's making remarkable progress?"

"Remarkable, Pat. You're a wonderful teacher." He sat down and began eating. Patricia came to sit beside him while Ling slumped in her armchair, glancing at both of them with hostile eyes.

"Are you tired, darling?"

He explained that everyone was on edge at Kebun Besar because of tomorrow's inspection. And had Patricia forgotten tomorrow night? She had promised to spend the day at the club to help get everything ready for the reception, along with the other planters' wives. The boys were unreliable in such circumstances.

"Of course I'm going," Patricia said. "Helene's supposed to pick me up tomorrow morning. We'll change at the club. Only . . ."

He thanked her, sententiously pointing out that nothing was more likely to predispose a great financier to a favorable report than a successful dinner.

". . . Only what worries me," she added, lowering her voice and glancing at Ling, "is that you'll be busy outside all day, and she'll be here alone."

"That'll be a good test. . . . After all, you can't take her to the club and introduce her to the count!"

Ling's presence in their house was no longer a mystery. Patricia had explained to everyone that she had found the girl living poverty-stricken in Singapore. Since her interest in charitable works for native children was well-known, and since the district was accustomed to her eccentricities, there had not been a breath of scandal. Nevertheless, Patricia regretfully admitted that it was a bit premature to be taking the girl to the club and introducing her into European society; she was not well enough acclimated yet. . . .

"After all," she decided with a sigh, "it won't be the first time we've both been out of the house."

"That's true"—Bernard looked hard at Ling—"only when we left her alone before, her leg hadn't completely healed. She had trouble walking." He shrugged his shoulders and told his wife he would be back very late. He must get back to the office now; Gopal was expecting him for a last look at the books.

Patricia had resumed her place beside Ling and was continuing the lesson.

"*Un an-i-mal c'louel,*" Ling said.

"*Crou-el,* dear. Listen carefully," Patricia repeated indulgently.

Near the door, Bernard watched them both with a certain tenderness.

"By the way, Pat," he said as he was leaving, "why teach her French and not English?"

75

"Does that mean my French isn't good enough?"

"Of course not, but maybe you wouldn't have to work so hard in English. Why French?"

Patricia condescendingly replied that it was quite naïve of him not to have guessed. The reason was perfectly obvious, after all. Ling was still in a savage state, at the zero point of civilization. Her education must be undertaken gradually, starting with the simpler stages.

10   Bernard quickly crossed the darkening plantation; he was in a hurry to reach his office. He knew how much importance the administrators attached to the theoretical organization of the business and the fascination they found in symbols, even independent of the results those symbols were supposed to express.

The clerks' hall was quiet, almost deserted. Only Mr. Gopal was there at his desk, lighted by a single lamp, behind a pile of folders and ledgers. Bernard went into his private office adjoining the main room. Before sitting at his desk he looked dourly at the portrait of the senior d'Erival, the company's founder. He shrugged his shoulders and summoned his faithful collaborator. Gopal arrived with his arms full of documents. Before beginning his final check, Bernard, without quite knowing why, asked him an unusual question: "What do you think of that portrait, Mr. Gopal?"

Mr. Gopal thought the portrait succeeded admirably in expressing the effect it was intended to convey. He expressed this opinion with care, his English correct and respectful. Bernard looked at him without speaking, then began to work. For a long time, in the silence of the night, they reviewed the columns of figures, the strange saw-toothed graphs, the striped diagrams on which the same result was represented in ten different ways until gradually all its reality evaporated. All these components derived ultimately from a monstrous distortion of the poetic faculty. The highest levels of modern enterprise imposed their accumulation of fancy around the brutal facts, perhaps to disguise their dryness, to provoke an artificial interest. Mr. Gopal had an instinctive sense of the meaning of such documents and presented them respectfully, one by one. Bernard managed to make himself pay suitable attention to each. They had often stayed here together, these two men, at nightfall, speaking to each other in a language incomprehensible to an outsider. Night created a deeper bond between them; at night Bernard could abandon the mask of the austere manager. "The yield per acre has increased, Mr. Gopal. I agree with you there," he said in reply to the old clerk's remark, "but the yield per man has fallen off, and our cash costs are especially high."

Mr. Gopal kept silent. He was well aware that cash costs were higher at Kebun Besar than the Company's theoretical norms stipulated. The whole office force knew it and felt vaguely guilty about the matter.

"Count d'Erival is certainly going to point out that

results on the Kedah plantations are more favorable. Have you seen the Company's comparative statistics?"

"I have seen them, sir," Mr. Gopal said. "But the country out there is flat and easier to work."

"The country is flat, all right," Bernard mused. "But the administrator of a great organization such as ours cannot take such details into consideration, Mr. Gopal."

"Certainly, sir," Mr. Gopal said.

Bernard stared at him again. The clerk's answers certainly left him feeling peculiar today. But the question of cash costs was too important; he must not be distracted by the philosophical meditations to which he felt himself strangely drawn. He recovered himself, leaned over another column, and asked, "How many trees did we replant this last quarter, Mr. Gopal?"

Mr. Gopal indicated the precise number.

"That's not so good." He was about to ask for further statistics when the telephone interrupted their work. It was Rawlinson.

"Two thousand trees destroyed during the last quarter, Comrade Wang," said Kim, leaning back and underlining the Chinese characters on the paper in front of him with his fingernail. "That's not very many."

They were sitting in Kim's office. Outside, the camp was quiet. The jungle imposed its nocturnal calm. Two storm lamps hanging from the rafters made the portrait of Mao Tse-tung gleam against the wall and illuminated a bamboo table on which stacks of papers were covered with columns, curves, stripes, and many-colored squares. Wang was standing behind his leader, handing him the ledgers one by one.

"It takes time to chop down a rubber tree, Comrade

Kim, and even so the curve is higher than it was the quarter before."

"They've done much better in the Kedah districts; I've just received the last comparative statistics. Look at them."

"That's flat country," Wang protested. "The sabotage commandos have a much easier time of it."

"That's not a good argument," Kim said severely.

He continued his final check before tomorrow's inspection. He knew how much importance the Party's great leaders, particularly Ho, attached to administrative organization. Besides, he had had good training in this field himself. Before joining the rebels he had worked as a secretary for a European firm. The things he had learned there had not been lost upon him; perhaps there were arts of Western civilization subtler than the symbolism of accounting and administration, but Kim had had no occasion to investigate them. Lacking all other sustenance, his alert mind had assimilated this nourishment. He had preserved a taste and a respect for documents. The brutal results of the raids and sabotage that formed the material basis of terrorist operations glowed for him with a romantic light, assuming a transcendental significance once they had been transformed into arithmetical or geometrical form. He knew how to calculate cash costs better than any other revolutionary leader.

Nevertheless, he felt a certain bitterness in discovering, on the very eve of inspection, that these costs had exceeded the permitted limits. The camp's budget was very hard to balance. The receipts from the raids were low, and profits from the various commando attacks were not satisfactory. As a result, expenses had increased, and from the moment of his arrival Comrade Ho would hardly be favorably impressed by his management.

He sighed, leaning over a column of figures in which the average of successful assassinations was calculated in relation to the number of partisans in the camp; the result was disappointing.

"The total will be higher by one unit," Wang offered timidly, "if we are successful tomorrow. I've written the figures in pencil here so that we can change them when the commandos return."

"One unit!" Kim sighed. "That will hardly affect the average."

"Nevertheless, an important unit, Comrade. It's a matter of quality as well."

"That's true," Kim admitted. "It's a matter of quality as well. I hope Comrade Ho takes that into account."

The operation Wang had just referred to had as its object the assassination of Count d'Erival, whose spies had informed them would be arriving at Kebun Besar tomorrow. Although this upset his plans somewhat for Comrade Ho's reception, Kim could not afford to miss such an opportunity. A small group led by Sen was to leave that night to ambush the administrator just before he reached the plantation.

His mind clogged with figures, Kim was about to make his final suggestions to his second in command when Sen suddenly burst into his office, gleaming with excitement and dragging behind him the Chinese clerk from Kebun Besar.

"Good news, Comrade Kim," Sen cried. "Ling is not dead!"

"Ling!"

Anxiously, Kim questioned the spy. The story seemed incredible, but he swore to its veracity. Not only was Ling alive, but she was not in the hands of the police. She was living—apparently free—in the French manager's bungalow, and the manager's wife was treating her like her own daughter. Better still, the American woman had gotten her a card of identity. The Chinese had learned this from another spy who worked in Rawlinson's office. He had even been able to obtain a copy of the identification photograph and had brought it along as proof.

It was Ling, there was no doubt about that. Ling was being kept as a hostage, of course. But why was she not in prison? It was incomprehensible. He would have to get more information. Meanwhile. . . . He met Sen's impatient eyes and looked away.

"We must abandon tomorrow's attack," he said slowly.

Sen looked at him sharply. It was obvious that he disapproved of his leader's decision.

"It was so well set up! . . . Then the commandos won't leave?"

"Yes," said Kim, after thinking a while longer. "They will leave right away, in order to be back by sunrise. But no attack. No violence. Those are my orders. We'll show them we're there all the same."

He described the new mission. Sen bowed, slightly reassured, and left to get his men. Kim walked back to his desk beneath the smiling portrait of Mao Tse-tung. He ordered Wang to consider the present average of successful assassinations as definitive, and to go over the figures in ink.

Ever since he had given in to his wife about Ling, Bernard had felt uneasy with Rawlinson. The police chief noticed a certain quaver in the manager's voice, but attributed his nervousness to tomorrow's inspection. Besides, that was what he himself was phoning about. He was worried too.

"Not so much as I am," Bernard interrupted.

"Probably—but at least that's why you're here." Rawlinson explained how he was involved, even though he was an Englishman and, in fact, had nothing to do with the Company in his official capacity. "It's quite simple. Every financier has connections in political and military circles. And the police are both political and military. First conclusion: if your great man should have an accident tomorrow, I'll be sacked; I've been politely informed. . . . You too? But I tell you, it's your job."

The second conclusion was that Rawlinson, in view of these recommendations from higher up, had decided to get together an escort that would convoy d'Erival to the plantation and not leave him alone for one second. "Two armored cars and a squadron of English troops. Is that all right with you?"

"Perfect," Bernard said. "It takes a big load off my shoulders. I've been worried about him."

"I'll bet you have!" the Englishman murmured. "If I were a terrorist, a man like that would be the first . . ." He did not finish his sentence, told Bernard he would call him tomorrow morning when the escort was leaving, and hung up.

Mr. Kha, Rawlinson's first secretary, was standing

behind him, silent and attentive, ready to hand him a ledger. Rawlinson stopped him with a gesture. He wanted a moment to think about Kebun Besar: for some time now the plantation had provided him with a number of enigmas to puzzle over.

He remembered the quaver in Bernard's voice at the beginning of the conversation. Of course he must be overwrought, but this wasn't the first time the chief of police thought he detected a certain uneasiness in Bernard's attitude toward him. There was something forced about his jocular tone. . . . Then there was that wounded terrorist who had mysteriously disappeared a month ago; the houseboy's embarrassment . . . and three weeks later Pat had decided to take in that Chinese girl. . . . Oh, it was quite like her to do such a thing, and the explanations about the lost papers were certainly plausible enough. Besides, Bernard had assumed responsibility for her. The guarantee of a European in a position like Bernard's made all suspicion absurd. He was being silly. To silence his conscience he had checked on whether Ling's family was really living in Singapore, without carrying his investigation any further, and had made out the card of identity. After all, Pat's gesture was a very generous one, susceptible of excellent political interpretations, and it was his duty to encourage her. An interesting experiment . . . but why did Bernard seem so uneasy?

He realized Mr. Kha was still standing behind him, and he felt guilty at having been so easily distracted. He was alone with his first secretary, an old Malay. His desk was covered with papers. On the wall behind him hung a framed portrait of a long-dead civil servant who seemed to stare into the room with an arrogant expression. Rawlinson and Mr. Kha often worked late into the evening, bringing the statistics and the ever more numerous documents concerning police activities in the district up to date. Mr. Kha always stood behind his chief, handing him a notebook, a chart, a list of figures from time to time, fetching them himself from the silent main office where the filing cabinets and the desks, a typewriter on each one, stood in straight, regular rows.

Rawlinson plunged back into the problem immediately confronting him, which was how to pay for tomorrow's escort. He heaved a sigh. This little sortie filled him with anxiety, though he was anything but a cowardly man. He could even joke about being the scapegoat and losing his job—accepting such a responsibility as one of the risks of the Service—should something happen to their distinguished guest. And it was certainly not fear of danger that made his knees tremble now, and his insides rumble, as Mr. Kha respectfully pointed to a column of figures. What frightened him was the fatal blow the cost of the escort would deal to his Service budget.

His district's cost of neutralizing the terrorists compared unfavorably with the rest of Malaya. He had recently received some comments on the subject, and the appearance of these further expenses in his accounts would certainly bring down some strong reprimands on his head. He had been obliged to request outside assistance, which was very expensive. Mr. Kha, who was aware of the problem and deplored the situation, echoed his sigh as he bent over a diagram indicating the costs of combating the terrorists in terms of manpower and district acreage covered.

"Headquarters are going to tell us again that results are better in the Kedah districts," Rawlinson murmured anxiously.

To console him, Mr. Kha pointed out that the Kedah districts were in flat country, which made police work considerably easier.

11   In the lantern-lit schoolroom, Comrade Ho was sitting in the schoolmaster's place on the dais. Next to him, his secretary was leafing through a dossier, and Kim was looking on in silence. Partisans were sitting on the benches and crouching on the floor around them. It was the moment when the great leader was formulating his observations and about to authorize a general discussion. The moment for the self-criticism session was near; Kim prepared himself for it.

The day had gone rather well for him. He had risen at dawn, when the jungle gibbons greet the sun with their long, harsh cries. The partisans were already busy. The commando raid sent to Kebun Besar had just returned, its mission completed, and all the men, under Sen's mocking supervision, had marched off to a stream to perform the toilet he had ordered.

"Rub, rub, rub!" Sen shouted. "Anyone who has mud

on his ears or grease under his nails will be punished. Pictures will be sent to the Party papers and all the women of the Popular Front will make fun of him. Rub, rub, rub!"

Kim had gone to meet Comrade Ho with a small escort, and had encountered him at the point agreed upon. The visitor had walked through the jungle for part of the night, accompanied by his bodyguard and followed by his private secretary, who was carrying a heavy briefcase and panting on the uphill stretches.

Comrade Ho had declared the camp to be in good order; the men's morale, instruction, and physical training were adequate. He had reserved this evening for examining various theoretical points. Outside, the jungle was as silent as usual. Most of its creatures make no noise. Only the gibbons, an hour before, had troubled its calm, greeting the sunset with long howls, as they had celebrated the dawn.

The leader worked through the discussion slowly, weighing his words. He took up several questions, one after another, in the order of their importance. The matter of cash costs had already been dealt with, and had constituted the object of rather severe criticism; Kim and the partisans had lowered their heads, sharing the responsibility of reproof. Comrade Ho was now attempting to mitigate the impression of severity he had just produced. Like all great leaders, he knew that an effective and intelligent authority must rely on a skillful mixture of reprimand and praise.

"The accounts are better kept than at the time of my last inspection," he said, "and the hygienic measures have been observed. That is progress." A murmur of satisfaction ran through the ranks. The secretary bent forward and whispered a few words in Ho's ear. Ho changed his expression again and mentioned the low percentage of successful assassinations. The remark was addressed to everyone, but it was obviously up to Kim to reply. He did so in a serious tone of voice, feeling that the moment had come. All eyes rested upon him as soon as he raised his voice.

"The number of successful assassinations would have been higher by one important unit this very day, Comrade Ho," he said, "if I had not decided against eliminating a capitalist visiting Kebun Besar."

"Decided against?"

"Yes, Comrade. I have decided to submit the case to you and to make my public self-criticism."

"Why did you change your plan?"

Gradually Ho assumed the accents of a judge interrogating a defendant, and the room took on the aspect of a court, with the little secretary as bailiff. The public was represented by the crowd of partisans. A rumor had flown through the camp that Kim was about to confess some delicate matter, and all the Chinese, passionate amateurs in casuistry and argument, hurried to hear the proceedings. Groups of latecomers had come in on tiptoe, and were crouching behind the rest. The room was full. At the door the sentries on duty occasionally thrust in their heads to hear what was going on.

"Well," said Kim, "at the moment the raid was about to leave, I learned that our Comrade Ling was in the manager's bungalow. The American woman has not handed her over to the police and seems to be protecting her."

"For what reason?"

"I do not know. Perhaps they are holding her as a hostage. It is a mystery. Until it is cleared up, I have decided to call off any violence planned against that plantation."

"What does Sen think of this decision?" Ho asked, turning toward the second in command.

"Sen thinks the attack should have been made," said the latter, not looking at Kim. "There will not be such an opportunity soon again. Ling is lost anyway, and our Party must ignore particular cases."

Ho remained silent for a long moment, frowning, while the inquisitive partisans tried to guess his thoughts. He looked around the first rows and pointed to a very young soldier. "What does Chao think of this decision?" It was the soldier who had thought of making a triumphal arch. Ho had stopped in front of him this morning during inspection, and having found his equipment in good order, had asked him his name. He had the leader's coquetry of showing off his excellent memory for details.

Chao stood up, thrilled by the honor. Nothing could have stopped him from speaking his mind. "Chao thinks Kim was right to call off the attack. The whites would have revenged themselves on Ling. Now perhaps she will be able to escape and return to camp."

Ho gave no sign of either praise or blame. He made a sign to Chao, who sat down again, and then turned toward Kim. "What does Kim think of this decision?"

Kim did not answer directly. A fair judgment must reckon with every aspect of a problem and leave no element in obscurity, even if some were to his own discredit. "First of all, Comrade Ho," he said slowly, "you

90

should know that I was intending to ask the Party to authorize my union with Ling. Is that an offense?"

"That is not an offense as such," Ho said dryly. "You know that. The Party encourages such unions. . . . But did this intention influence your decision?"

They had reached the critical point in the discussion, as the partisans well knew. Everyone held his breath, anxiously awaiting Kim's reply. It came as a disappointment. Since the night before, Kim had expected this question, and had put it to himself far more severely than Ho could have, desperately seeking the truth in a frantic examination of his conscience. He had not been able to arrive at any certainty as to his guilt; instead he was overwhelmed by the dawning realization that an objective self-criticism is an impossible operation for the mind. Conscience-stricken at having to condemn himself unfairly one way or the other, Kim lowered his head and murmured, "I don't know."

Ho did not change his stern expression and ended the discussion in unyielding tones. "You were wrong, Comrade Kim. A leader of the Popular Army must in no case take his private feelings into account."

A slight tremor ran through the ranks and immediately subsided. Kim was liked and respected, but after having weighed the facts of the matter, all the partisans understood that Ho's arguments were very powerful.

The inspector was about to raise another question when a sudden movement swept through the groups near the door. Ho, annoyed, lifted his head, but, hearing even louder exclamations, he realized that something extraordinary had occurred. A name was whispered by fifty mouths, then spoken aloud with mounting feeling: "Ling, Ling . . . Ling!" One of the sentries cleared a path to the dais and announced, "Ling is back!"

She made a pitiful appearance as she followed the sentry in, her feet bleeding, her tattered pajamas covered with mud. Kim made a sudden movement, as if he were about to rush to her side, but at once sat down again. He must preserve his presence of mind in every circumstance, especially when the inspector was watching him. He made a sign and the disturbance died away. The soldiers returned to their places. Ling advanced toward the dais and stumbled. Kim told her to be seated. In a few broken sentences she indicated that she was merely out of breath. As soon as she had gotten her bearings, she had run all the way back to camp. She would soon recover her strength. Everyone stirred in eagerness to hear her story.

But first there was one essential question to be settled. Even the humblest partisans sensed it, and everyone was staring at Ho, who remained silent and thoughtful. It was young Chao who found in his youth and enthusiasm the courage to express the common wish. He stood up without being asked, looked straight into Ho's eyes, and asked, "May Chao speak?"

A profound silence greeted this boldness, for everyone knew what the boy was going to say. Ho, who had also guessed, seemed disconcerted for a moment, then smiled. "Speak."

"Ling has returned," Chao said. "Kim was right. Kim is cleared."

The silence expressed the dramatic tension that held all minds prisoner. Ho, in his turn, seemed plunged in an abyss of introspection. Finally he spoke, in his most solemn voice.

"You are right, Comrade Chao," he said slowly. "Kim was right to call off the attack. Kim is cleared."

This announcement was received by an enthusiastic murmur, followed by another silence. It was still not enough. There had to be a clearer confession. Realizing this, Ho continued: "I am sorry I disapproved. It was I who was wrong to blame Kim, when he was in the right. I have judged too quickly. I accuse myself of having done so."

That was how it should be. These were the very words they were waiting for, and several young soldiers applauded wildly. Kim attempted to silence this outburst, but the great leader Ho prevented him with a gesture. A storm of bravos paid homage for a moment to the tribunal's wisdom and objectivity. Then Ling began her story.

12   When Patricia had left her to spend the
day at the club, Ling decided to act.

The chief obstacle was the houseboy, this dog who
fawned before his mistress, and to whom his mistress
had made a thousand recommendations concerning her.
Now the creature spied on her every movement. At
first she had violently abused him, in Chinese, but he
was not affected by her words. He confined himself to
answering: "Speak French, Missi, *mem* says to learn
quickly," with a placidity that left her trembling with
rage.

So she had changed her tactics. Pretending to resign
herself to his custody, she had asked him, as a favor,
to help her pass the time by turning on the radio, and
while he was on his knees manipulating the buttons
she had knocked him out with a bottle. He had fallen
without a sound. That was how the strong and clever

soldiers of the Popular Army always triumphed over traitors. She regretted not having cut his throat before leaving, but she had not a second to lose.

She had run away without taking time to get dressed, still wearing her pajamas, creeping behind the bungalow to avoid the Malays. For several days beforehand she had managed to orient herself more or less, and she quickly reached the edge of the jungle, but at a point unfamiliar to her. She wasted time looking for the paths leading to the camp, and got lost several times. She was not in training for long-distance running, and her wound had weakened her. When she finally found the landmarks she knew, she lost her head for joy and began to run until she was out of breath. But her weakness had passed; she was forgetting her fatigue at the notion of taking her place again among her comrades. Her time among the whites was only a bad dream.

"And that's the whole story," she concluded, after describing how Patricia had treated her. "Ling is not grateful. The American woman's heart is full of selfish thoughts. She petted me like an animal, to tame me and make me fond of her. She tried to keep me with her, to make me into a girl like those of her rotten world. . . . She wanted me to adore her God, and to put rouge on my lips," she added in disgust.

At the dinner given by the partisans in his honor, Ho invited Ling to sit next to him. Kim and the secretary also sat at his table. The other partisans crouched on the ground around them. Supplementary rations of rice from the camp's reserves were added to the menu, as well as several bottles of Chinese wine, brought by the illustrious visitor's bodyguard.

Ho listened to Ling's story without interruption and

appeared to be reflecting deeply upon it. "And the American woman obtained papers for you?" he asked at last.

"Here is my card of identity. Ling has no need of it." She was about to tear it up, but Ho stopped her with a sudden gesture. Kim watched him with dawning anxiety.

"Ling must return to the whites," said the great leader after a silence.

Kim could not repress a movement of protest. He had been fearing such a decision for the last few moments. Ling paled and remained silent.

"Among the whites, Ling will serve our cause even better than here. Ling is intelligent and wily. She will gain the whites' confidence. She will listen to their conversations. She will become our best spy. Since the American woman has taken her under her protection, Ling will pretend to be converted to her ideas."

"For how long?" Kim implored.

"As long as she will be useful to our cause," Ho replied dryly.

"Ling is ready to go back now," Ling said, after having exchanged a tender, pained look with Kim.

Such duties are painful to carry out, but the mission's importance was obvious. Nevertheless, the girl was exhausted, and in addition it was too late for her to return without her absence being noticed. Ho decided she should rest for several hours, and then return to the plantation early in the morning. It would be best for her to confess her flight to the American woman. She would say she had left on a whim; that she had thought it over, felt remorse, and remembering how she had been treated, had decided to come back, repentant. Ho

exchanged several whispered words with his secretary;
the little man was apparently a counsellor in all affairs
of such delicacy. Together they decided that the American woman would be flattered by Ling's return, and
that she would impose her will on her husband, should
he have any objections. Judging by Ling's account of
the couple's behavior, they believed that the incident
would then be closed. There was the matter of the
houseboy she had knocked out, but Ling was certain he
had been merely stunned. Here, too, the American
woman seemed to have enough influence in the bungalow so that the incident would be forgotten. In a tone
of intense conviction, Ho concluded, "It is heaven itself that has put this American woman in our path."

"Or my evil genius," Kim murmured darkly.

"You are forgetting that if it had not been for the
American woman, Ling would be dead."

"Perhaps that would be better."

Comrade Ho pretended not to hear this last mani-
festation of bad temper. The dinner was over. All the
important questions had been settled. He stood up and
pronounced the little speech that Chinese ceremonial
politeness requires even in the rather special circumstances created by terrorism and life in the jungle. He
reminded his listeners that his criticisms had been inspired entirely by a concern for their general progress
and the triumph of their cause. On the whole, he was
pleased with the work accomplished by the camp under Kim's leadership. He added that their leaders in
Peking were aware of the difficult conditions under
which they were working, and were proud of their
heroism.

A wave of acclamation greeted these last words. Ho

sat down again and made a sign to the soldiers of his bodyguard. They opened a chest they had brought with them and began distributing presents to the comrades.

At the planters' club the dinner was almost over. The houseboys were serving champagne. Everyone was waiting for the moment when Count d'Erival would stand up to speak the inevitable words bringing the dinner to a close.

Bernard was exhausted but quite pleased. The day had been a good one, all in all. . . .

It had begun so badly! What a turn the morning had given him. He could still feel his heart beating at the thought. Up at dawn after a night of bad dreams, he had gone to the office where the clerks were already at their desks, stiff in the starched shirts that crackled at each movement.

"A great day, Mr. Gopal," he said, trying to introduce a little jocular humanity into the strained atmosphere.

"A very great day, sir," Mr. Gopal had gravely replied.

He could scarcely expect a different reaction from Mr. Gopal. Discouraged by this model employee's dignity and reserve, Bernard waited for Rawlinson's telephone call. The Englishman's tone consoled him a little. "Hello, Bernard! . . . Just wanted to let you know the circus is on the road. Squadron, armored cars, everything except the elephants and the music."

"And the clowns, of course."

"Oh, we've plenty of clowns, don't worry about that,"

answered the police chief, grimly looking out of his office window where their distinguished guest was taking his place in the sumptuous car between two trucks full of soldiers.

At that moment Bernard felt a great burst of sympathy for Rawlinson. He hung up and, accompanied by Robert Jourdain, went to meet the convoy at the plantation gate.

Here catastrophe was only narrowly avoided. As they turned onto the road beyond the bridge, they discovered the terrorists' latest exploit: all the trees along the road were hung with insulting inscriptions in red paint two feet high, in Western letters Comrade Wang had taught the cleverest of the commandos how to make. Fortunately, after hastily driving off to intercept the convoy, Bernard and Robert had been able to re-enter the plantation by a different gate.

Just now, while all eyes were fixed on the Count's massive, seated silhouette, Robert Jourdain was explaining to Rawlinson the reasons for this detour. He was speaking quietly but passionately, his voice betraying the emotion he, too, had felt. "Go home, go home, go home! On every single tree. Imagine the two hedges of 'Go home' he would have had to ride between—two parallel lines meeting at infinity, you know. . . . Enough to kill him, I should think!"

There were similar vandalisms all over the plantation. The rest of the morning had been spent making ingenious detours to avoid offending the visitor. Thanks to God and Robert Jourdain, who had preceded the convoy, the Count had suspected nothing.

"I wonder what's gotten into them," Rawlinson said

thoughtfully. "A grenade or a little machine-gun fire I expected—something of the kind. But this? It's almost as if they were developing a sense of humor!"

"If he had seen it, he would never have admitted that such a thing could have been done by terrorists. We would all have gotten the sack."

"Now that you mention it, I wonder . . ." Rawlinson murmured.

"Wonder what?"

"Well, come on, now, just between you and me, who *did* have such a wonderful idea out here at Kebun Besar? I can keep a secret. . . ."

"You!—" Robert Jourdain began furiously. Then he grew calm again, and thoughtful. "After all, John, take the first person you come across by chance, among everyone here tonight, and I'll bet he'd be capable of having written those things."

"It could be very serious," Rawlinson murmured, thoughtful too. "Is a certain 'community of opinion' being established between them and us? Well, speak for yourself," he added suddenly, changing his tone. "You French are all so disrespectful of authority. As for me, you know, I would never, never have written or spoken such a thing—'Go home'!"

They were obliged to speak lower still, for a silence had fallen upon the table. In the place of honor, Count d'Erival had stood up to make his remarks.

"So!" whispered Robert. "What would *you* have said?"

"*Go to hell!*" Rawlinson answered in a fierce whisper.

And they stopped talking in order to listen to the speech that Occidental tradition requires to create a certain relaxation of the nerves. Count d'Erival told them that it was a leader's role to criticize, but that on the whole he had been pleased by his visit to the Company's plantations. He finished by proposing a toast to the great family they comprised and assured them that the Board of Directors in Europe was proud of their work and the heroic struggle they were carrying on day by day.

Comrade Ho looked around him, satisfied with the impression made by the gifts his men had finished distributing. The wide-eyed partisans were showing their prizes to one another. There were notebooks, textbooks, pens, and other school supplies. He pointed out that these objects had been made in the People's Republic of China, in the first factory of its kind, opened only a few months before. This announcement provoked a final wave of enthusiasm and a storm of applause.

Then the partisans left the schoolroom, discussing the celebration. Ho turned to Kim and offered him a package the secretary had just taken out of his briefcase.

"This is for you, Comrade Kim. In spite of my criticisms, I think you are a good leader."

It was a portrait of Mao Tse-tung, with a signed dedication. Kim was overwhelmed. "Thank you, Comrade," he stammered. "Ling and I are glad to yield to necessity. We will wait until the Liberation to be united."

Ho retired into the cabin that had been detailed for his use; he was to leave early the next morning. There were other distant camps to inspect and other delicate missions to accomplish. Kim and Ling looked at each other in silence.

"You must get some sleep, little sister," Kim said at last. "I'll watch over you." He led her to his own tent, put her to bed on his own mats, and covered her with his single blanket.

"I must leave at dawn."

"I promise to wake you."

"Oh, Kim, Kim," she cried suddenly, "I'm afraid of going back to live with the whites. I'm afraid of the American woman and her caresses and her smiles, and the smiles I have to return. I would be less afraid if they had told me to cut her throat."

"I, too, little sister," Kim said, clenching his fists in his excitement, "I, too, would prefer to attack a whole squadron of Gurkhas by myself than to see you go back to the American woman!"

"It's for the Liberation, big brother," she murmured, closing her eyes.

"For the Liberation, little sister."

Ling had fallen asleep, her strength exhausted. Kim crouched near the door and watched over her all night long.

PART THREE

13   Bernard looked up from his newspaper and watched contentedly as Patricia and Ling, sitting side by side, devoted themselves to the daily French lesson, both women equally absorbed. The sight affected him a little more every day. He realized that for some time he had been finding a new interest in his family life, perhaps in the observation of the relationships destiny had produced between two human beings so different from each other.

It was evening. The houseboy had cleared the table and disappeared, leaving the living-room bay window wide open at Bernard's request. It was not very prudent: anyone might approach the house as far as the edge of the garden under cover of the trees, and their three silhouettes were easy targets; but Bernard felt inclined to optimism and even insouciance this evening.

For six months, ever since the administrator's visit, the terrorists had not shown a sign of life.

After her flight, which they could not help forgiving in view of her repentance and her promises of loyalty, Ling seemed on the right track at last. She had made great progress in French. She studied with an intelligence and an application matched only by Patricia's patience.

Just now she was reciting one of La Fontaine's fables. Her accent was quite good, although she still stumbled occasionally on the r's.

> *" 'Et que pa' consequent*
> *En aucune façon*
> *Je ne puis t'oublier sa boisson . . .' "*

"*Troubler, trou . . .*" Patricia broke in.

"*Tu la troubles, lui dit cette bête c'uelle . . .*"

"*Crou-elle, crou,* dear," Patricia continued.

"*Cru-elle,* darling," Bernard interrupted, moved by the girl's efforts.

"*Cru-elle,*" repeated Ling, almost correctly.

Patricia shrugged her shoulders, ignoring her husband's triumphant glance. She closed the book, congratulated Ling on her good memory, and began to question her to discover whether she had understood the fable's meaning, and its moral in particular. Morality played an important part in her pedagogic program.

Yet Ling dreaded having to explain such matters, and it was just this part of the lesson that was a painful ordeal for her. She remained silent for a long while, her face impassive.

"Now, Ling," Patricia resumed in an encouraging tone, "what does the author mean when he says '*La raison du plus fort est toujours la meilleure?'* I told you about that just the other day."

It was purely a question of memory. Ling answered in a monotonous singsong, repeating what Patricia had told her: "Those who enjoy power always arrange matters so as to give their tyranny an appearance of justice." Patricia looked delighted. Bernard, who was watching Ling closely, wondered what her secret thoughts might be, and asked permission to question her in his turn.

"Do you think it's right that things should be that way—that those in power always manage to have right on their side?"

Ling reacted violently. "Not at all, very bad, on the contrary," she cried, her voice no longer that of the diligent schoolgirl. And almost hysterically she added: "And the judgment of history ends up by exposing the tyrants' lies. The oppressed people always succeed in overturning their power and destroying them."

This was a remembrance of lessons learned before those she had received from the American woman. Bernard murmured, "Yes . . . of course! Bravo!" scarcely concealing his grin. Patricia interrupted brightly to underline the fact that if serious injustices had occurred in the past, there existed today nations both strong *and* just which made use of their power only to protect the weaker ones and to assist them to raise themselves to their own level. "And what," she asked, "is responsible for this tremendous progress in the attitude of both individuals and nations?"

"The emergence of the proletariat," Ling countered.

Again she had spoken instinctively. If she dreaded these sessions, it was because she frequently allowed herself to be carried away by her faith, at the risk of self-betrayal. She stopped as if caught in some reprehensible act, but Patricia was careful not to administer a direct rebuke.

"Yes, of course . . . perhaps," she said, "but still . . . Ling, I have explained it to you."

Ling resumed her obedient singsong, making great efforts to conceal her scorn. "This progress is due to the simultaneous development of the democratic spirit and of Christian morality," she chanted; "to the ideal of kindness, charity, and brotherhood which Christ was the first to preach and which the civilized nations are today spreading throughout the world."

Patricia was too intelligent not to notice the change in the girl's tone; but like many teachers, she believed that the spirit ultimately disengaged itself from the letter, the conviction from the convention. She announced that she was satisfied with the lesson and helped her pupil to bring it to an end.

"Fine, Ling. And what did Christ say?"

"Love one another," Ling continued obediently, with an almost imperceptible quaver in her voice. "Love thy neighbor as thyself for love of Me."

The little scene was not a new one. It had been repeated quite often, and Bernard, when his wife triumphantly flashed him a look, replied good-humoredly that Ling's progress was remarkable. Rawlinson had made the same remark when, having stopped at the bungalow for a drink, he watched a similar session. He had merely added, in his well-behaved little-boy's tone, which was famous throughout the district, "It's extraordinary, Pat. She's beginning to discover our century's most stupefying miracle. And so am I."

"What miracle?"

"The miracle, Pat, that in our time it is precisely the nations in power who are perfect from every point of view. I had never realized that before tonight."

There was not much to answer to this. Patricia confined herself to shrugging her shoulders, and now, this evening, received her husband's ambiguous smile in the same fashion. She knew she would triumph in the end.

The lesson over, Ling asked permission to leave the room. "May I go to bed now, *mem?*"

The houseboy's name for Patricia, although it offended the girl, was still the one that came instinctively to her lips when she addressed her instructor. The latter insisted once again that she call her Pat, like everyone else, and also pointed out that Ling had no need to ask permission to leave the room.

"I'm taking the chest into my room—Pat. I'll pack the bags."

Patricia thanked her. Ling was referring to some presents for an orphanage in Singapore that Patricia visited once a week and to which she took Ling. The practice of charity was the second principle of Patricia's instruction: the two were to go into the city the next day. There were also several presents for Ling's family, which the girl herself now undertook to distribute. With the houseboy's help, she moved the big chest full of packages and two empty suitcases into her room.

The Delavignes stared after her, remaining silent and thoughtful for a moment before Bernard began to speak. "She's still rather . . ."

"I'll manage to transform her altogether," Patricia broke in. "But it takes patience—and tact, dear, tact. That's the trouble with you French whenever you come in contact with underprivileged races. You must realize that these poor people need an ideal. They think they've found it in Communism. You have to show them their error, and at the same time give them something else to believe in. You'll come over to my side one of these days. . . . Besides," she remarked, "you're already behaving better in your dealings with the natives."

Bernard protested vaguely. She pointed out that for several weeks he had not sworn at the houseboy or at the Malays. As for Ling, Patricia was really grateful to him for that—his attitude toward her had been perfect.

He was going to protest again, but upon reflection decided his wife was right. For some time he had felt inexplicably indulgent toward everyone. He shrugged his shoulders grumpily, walked over to the bay window, and stood in a reverie, absorbed in contemplation of the dark hills. After all, it was not his nature to be playing the local adjutant all the time; especially when things were going well on the plantation, as they were now. . . . Next year he would be up for a six months' leave in France, the last before retirement. It was something agreeable to look forward to. They would have to take Ling with them; Pat would never be willing to leave her behind. She was talking of adopting the girl— a Chinese, and from the rebels! If anyone ever found out! But perhaps Ling would really become quite civilized; she seemed to be off to a good start now.

All things considered, he had only favorable expectations, especially since he had heard nothing more of the terrorists. He pointed this out to Patricia, who had come to stand next to him at the window.

"It's the first result of our good deed, dear," she declared. "They can't be unaware of the fact that we've taken Ling in instead of handing her over to the police."

"That's for sure. They have spies all over the place. It even worries me . . ."

"And they're expressing their gratitude by sparing Kebun Besar."

He gave a skeptical snort, then thought about the matter further. After all, there might be an element of truth in what Pat was saying. For several weeks now he had been strangely inclined to pay attention to some of his wife's remarks, to think them over instead of laughing them off. Peace, he mused, always rests on a harmonious combination of benevolence and intimidation. Maybe Pat's ingenuity contained a certain share of wisdom? He knew from his own informants that the terrorists were not even extorting money from the workers, as they had in the past. . . .

"In any case, Pat . . ."

"Yes, dear?"

"In any case," he declared, stretching voluptuously, still facing the sleeping plantation, "Kebun Besar is a pleasant enough place for the rest of us when there are no troublemakers around . . ."

She pressed close against him and reminded him that all Malaya could be like this if the Europeans exerted a little good will. Then they began talking about Ling again. She was relying heavily on the practice of charity as an element in the girl's re-education.

"When we're with the orphanage children, I can see a real enthusiasm in her—I've noticed it two or three times already. It's by taking pity on the poor and the humble that she'll forget the law of the jungle and learn to love her neighbor."

"To love her neighbor, yes . . ." Bernard murmured, still musing, ". . . I suppose so. She's certainly less wild, gentler. . . . But all the same, Pat," he added, smiling, "you ought to amuse her a little, too. She's only a girl. Why don't you show her some aspects of our civilization that are a little less austere? Your good works are all very well, but . . ."

Pat replied that she had been thinking the same thing, that Ling wasn't destined exclusively to be a patroness. Tomorrow she would distribute her "good works," as Bernard so ironically called them, in the morning, and the afternoon she would keep for amusement.

"That's a fine idea!"

"She really has a heart of gold," Patricia concluded. "Ever since she's rediscovered her mother and her sisters, she loves helping them."

Bernard remarked rather sharply that he had found this out for himself, since it was costing him a pretty penny for her to do so. Ever since Ling had made up with her family, Pat was constantly asking him for money. "Between your orphans and that family of hers, darling, we capitalists are going to be on our uppers."

"Darling, you don't seriously begrudge me the money?"

Her tone was disarming. He looked at her affectionately and admitted that as a matter of fact he had never dreamed of denying her a penny.

"It makes those poor people so happy," Patricia continued with an artless smile it was difficult to resist.

He put his hands on her shoulders and looked at her again.

"It makes those poor people so happy. . . . And you,

darling," he continued, in a tone in which tenderness and admiration were mingled, "it gives you such pleasure to play the good fairy!"

"Yes, dear, it does," Patricia admitted, kissing him.

14   Alone in her room, Ling suffered a momentary lapse: she had no difficulty resisting Patricia's lessons as long as they were concerned with positive matters, like the characteristics of a language—this both interested and diverted her—but the American woman's qualitative judgments and her commentaries on morality produced in her a nervous tension that left her limp with fatigue. She sat down on her bed, resting her head on her hands, dizzy and dismayed. Then she stood up, tore off her housecoat so that she was wearing only pajamas—the only clothing she had that did not repel her—violently rubbed her lips to wipe off the lipstick she sometimes used to please Patricia, smoothed her hair, turned her head toward the living room, and half murmured, half spat in disgust: "Pigs!"

Somewhat comforted, she listened to the noises of the bungalow. When Patricia and Bernard had gone to bed, she stood up and began working on a mysterious task. She opened the chest the houseboy had brought, put the two suitcases on her bed, and spread out on the floor a great square cloth. After having locked her door from the inside, she began to unwrap the presents intended for the orphans and her family.

The first package contained children's clothes. She made a disappointed face and an angry gesture. "Nothing good for the comrades there," she murmured. She stuffed them regretfully into a suitcase and next took out a bundle of napkins of different sizes. She looked more satisfied at this, selected the largest ones, folded them carefully, and put them on the square cloth. The rest were tossed into the suitcase.

After this she took her time, and carefully deliberated before choosing among the comestibles: cans of powdered milk, chocolate, tea, butter. She worked hard, frowning as she did when she was writing a difficult French theme for Patricia. Finally a good share of the best provisions joined the rest of the articles in the carefully prepared bundle on the floor. She divided the rest among the valises with a sigh.

She continued the distribution in the same way. When the chest was almost empty, her face lighted up as she noticed at the bottom various medical supplies, including a box of quinine. This was more precious than gold for the comrades. She took a huge share of it, smiling at the thought of how surprised Kim would be when he saw it. There had been a severe attack of malaria in the camp.

She was finished. She closed the suitcases, after having wrapped the articles in several layers of paper so they would take up an impressive amount of space.

This was unnecessary anyway, for Patricia trusted her and never checked her work. To the bundle for the comrades she added other provisions she had hidden in her closet, supplies she stole daily from the refrigerator. She knotted the four corners of the cloth together, turned out the light, and waited again in the darkness.

After about an hour, she noiselessly walked down the hall, listening first at Pat's door, then at Bernard's. Both were sound asleep, since they were accustomed to getting up very early. She returned to her room, locked the door from the inside again, opened her window, and leaped down into the garden. She stood stockstill a moment, on the alert. The *mata-matas* couldn't see her from their post—besides, they were always asleep after dark—but she mistrusted the houseboy, her enemy. Reassured, she crossed the garden stealthily, reached the strip of jungle, and disappeared into the obscurity of the rubber grove.

She knew the way well now. She had gone to the meetingplace every week for six months. Far from the bungalow, she walked faster, then began to run. Soon she reached the path at the edge of the jungle and stopped, out of breath, near a giant tree that towered over the forest. She gave the signal and repeated it several times at regular intervals. Her eyes shone with pleasure when she heard the reply. A silhouette crossed the path and approached. It was Kim. He looked at her a long time without touching her.

"Is everything all right?"

"Too good," Ling sighed.

"Too good?"

"They're all very nice," Ling burst out angrily,

". . . and she—she never stops caressing me, as if I were a puppy."

"I know," he said, taking her hands in his, "it's hard to bear."

They remembered that they were soldiers, and Ling made her report. First of all she gave him the bundle. "All I could steal . . . there's quinine in it."

He congratulated her on her skill. She took from her pocket a piece of paper on which she had written all the information she could glean during the week from her benefactors' conversations, from the club parties she was now permitted to attend, or from their visits to Singapore. Kim ran his eyes over the report, put it in his own pocket, and thanked her again, admiringly.

"My little sister Ling is subtle as the musk deer," he said.

It was one of his favorite compliments. Thanks to her work, he was up to date on all police movements in the district.

They could not linger. As he was about to leave her, Ling noticed Kim's preoccupied expression. He admitted that the terrorist operations were not going very well. The government was intensifying its repressive action, and after several failures, a number of partisans had admitted feeling discouraged. They would have to show their power by several strong attacks. The Cause required it. But they needed arms and ammunition, and these tools could only be procured for gold. Fortunately he had just driven a favorable bargain during the last few days: a shipment of machine guns which a Malay sergeant had undertaken to get for him before deserting. But he needed cash, too. The camp's treasury was virtually empty.

"How much do you need?"

"Five hundred dollars."

She thought quickly. "Tomorrow I'm going to Singapore with the American woman. Can Kim send someone here the next night? Perhaps Ling will find the money."

He looked at her, delighted, and asked her for no explanations, knowing that he could count on her to produce miracles when the Cause was in need of them. He assured her he would be only too happy to come himself to meet her. They left each other, taking their separate ways.

15　　　The American Ford was heading toward Singapore, driven by a Malay *syce* in a white uniform and the classic black velvet cap. Patricia and Ling were in the back seat; Ling in a European dress instead of the pajamas she insisted on wearing in the bungalow. Following Patricia's instructions, the *syce* had taken the road along the sea, which was longer and in worse condition but more picturesque than the other.

Ling, apparently preoccupied, did not once look at the landscape. Since the day before she had been plotting how to get hold of some money, and she silently cursed the woman beside her who kept glancing at her out of the corner of her eye, distracting her from her calculations.

"Don't you think the sea is beautiful today, Ling?"

"Very pretty."

Ling fell silent again. Patricia did not insist on making her talk. The road left the sea and the car turned down the long, straight avenue lined with Malay *kampongs* half buried in a forest of attap and coconut palms. A canal followed alongside, its bank enlivened by fishermen, boys swimming, and women in sarongs washing clothes. Everyone waved greetings as the car passed, and Patricia waved back happily.

"You have to get away from the towns to see the Malays as they really are," she remarked. "Look, Ling, how friendly and natural they seem. Why don't we try to know them better? That's what I always tell Bernard."

But Ling felt only scorn for the Malays. She thought they were base, lazy, retarded, without ambition, and ready to lick the hand of whatever invaders happened to be in their country, provided their vegetable lives were not disturbed. She forced herself to look at them, again murmured, "Yes, very pretty," and plunged back into her calculations.

"Dear," Patricia sighed, disappointed, "you don't seem any more interested than Bernard and the rest of the Europeans out here!"

In Singapore they went straight to the orphanage, which was run by French nuns. Ling seized the heavier of the two suitcases, refusing all offers of assistance, and carried it to the sister in charge of supplies. When she returned to the courtyard, the customary ritual, which for her was the equivalent of a refined torture, was about to begin.

The children were lined up in two rows to greet and thank the American lady. Patricia passed them in review and insisted on speaking a few kind words to each one. She believed she must concern herself with their minds as well as with their physical health, and that the French sisters, in spite of their devotion, did not attach enough importance to the children's moral education. Since most of the orphans were Chinese, it was Ling who served as interpreter. They recited the lessons they had learned and, from Ling's point of view, gave every evidence of a vileness and servility that revolted her.

"Aren't they adorable?" cried Patricia, stroking their cheeks.

"Ado'able," Ling answered. She despised these children and instinctively adopted her worst accent in speaking about them.

"Where do you come from?" Patricia asked, stopping in front of a ten-year-old boy with evasive eyes.

Ling translated the question and, coldly, the answer. The child had come from Perak. His father had been killed in a raid after having joined a terrorist group. Patricia, moved to tears, implored the child not to harbor bitterness in his heart toward them, and he replied, as did the rest, that he was happy to have been adopted by the whites and that his gratitude would be eternal. Ling was on the point of screaming with anger.

It was already late in the morning when, their duties toward their less fortunate brothers accomplished, Patricia and Ling found themselves back in the Ford. They told the chauffeur to drive them to the center of town where Patricia had to run several uninteresting errands, leaving Ling to go see her family alone. They would meet at the Raffles Hotel for lunch.

Ling had hoped for this moment of freedom, which would favor her plans. The *syce* entered the labyrinth of the Chinese quarter and stopped, his expression one of disgust, in front of the wretched house where the girl's family lived.

She walked in, the suitcase in her hand, with her customary distaste. She could not set aside the nauseating memories of her childhood, and felt only contempt for her mother. But her role among the whites made it necessary for her to simulate a certain filial piety nevertheless.

Her mother was there, in the single room of the ground floor, surrounded by six sickly, ill-dressed children, her brothers and sisters, for whom her affection was no greater than for her mother. Her grandmother, an old, wizened Chinese woman, toothless and ailing, was wedged into a shaky chair. As usual, her eyes fastened on Ling from the moment she entered and did not move from her face until she left. Ling was not sure which she detested more—this wordless stare, or her mother's bitter jeremiads.

There was no effusiveness—there never was. The children merely formed a greedy circle around the suitcase. The mother, a graceless Chinese woman with shifty eyes, pushed them back and approached. Ling hated her hypocritical manners in front of Patricia and the act she put on to gain her sympathy.

"The *mem* has not come?"

Ling explained quickly that Patricia was busy elsewhere and had told her to bring several presents; then, finding nothing else to add, she opened the suitcase. The mother shoved away the children again as they were rushing forward, and one by one patted the objects that had escaped Ling's previous choice. The grandmother, forgotten in her corner, stretched out her neck, trying to see too.

"Is that all?" Ling's mother spoke in a spiteful tone, and stared suspiciously at her daughter. It was apparent that she did not trust her at all. "The American *mem* has promised many things."

"That's all," Ling said dryly. "The *mem* talks much, like all the whites."

The mother muttered further recriminations, her fingers searching out every corner of the suitcase. She seized Ling's dress between her skinny fingers and enviously estimated its worth. "Ling is dressed like a white *mem*. Ling lacks nothing. She eats as much as she wants and leaves her family to starve. If Ling knew how to ask, the American *mem* would give much more."

Ling answered furiously that she was not a beggar.

"And this? Ling knows how to beg for herself."

She pointed to the girl's necklace. It was a present Patricia had given her several days ago as a reward for good behavior and diligence in her lessons. Ling pulled away, stepped back, tore off the necklace, and thrust it in her bag which she was holding close against her. This action inspired a new litany of bitter reproaches, while the old grandmother watched the scene in silence, her eyes riveted to Ling's face.

"Your grandmother is sick; much fever."

Scornfully, Ling indicated what remained of the medical supplies. Then she decided she had been there long enough; she felt herself choking with shame at the thought of belonging to this family. She said she was in a great hurry and left at once, almost running, pursued by lamentations and the intolerable stare of the old woman, who attempted to stammer a few words as the girl was disappearing.

Ling told the *syce* she had another errand in the neighborhood. The man seemed surprised, but Patricia had insisted that all her servants obey the *missi* as if Ling's orders were her own. So the chauffeur drove the splendid car through the miserable streets with an increasingly evident disdain. She told him to stop at the corner of a filthy alley and to wait for her there, which he did without saying a word.

Ling walked a few steps down the alley, made sure the Malay could no longer see her, and ducked into a dark shop filled with various objects. An old Chinese merchant stared at her questioningly but showed little surprise. She opened her bag and took out the necklace.

"How much?" she asked.

A close bargaining followed. The Chinese offered one hundred dollars. Ling demanded five hundred. She ended by accepting two hundred and fifty, already scheming to get hold of the rest of the money.

When she reached the Raffles, Patricia, who was sitting alone on the terrace in front of a gin, looked up and signaled to her. Intimidated, Ling had to cross the whole bar to join her. It was cocktail time, and the room was full of drinkers: general-staff officers, businessmen, planters on leave, boat passengers in transit. She was uncomfortable in her European dress and felt that everyone was looking at her. As a matter of fact, many men turned to glance at her when she passed, and the Chinese waiters stared at her strangely.

During this moment she stiffened her features into an agonized expression. She had already reddened her eyes by rubbing them hard in the car. She hated the comedy she would have to play, for it reminded her unpleasantly of her mother's snivelings. But the higher interest of the Cause justified these miserable means.

Noticing her expression, Patricia questioned her with concern.

"My little sister," she finally admitted, after pretending to hesitate for some time,"—she never stops coughing. The hospital doctor has said she must go to the mountains right away."

"Well?"

"My mother has no money," Ling said, lowering her head.

This distress could scarcely leave her benefactress' heart unmoved. "How terrible, dear. How much do you need?"

"No, no," Ling protested. "My mother has said not to accept. The *mem* is too good. Ling, too, is ashamed."

Overwhelmed by such sensitivity, Patricia spoke with the gentle authority to which she was accustomed in such cases, and which it was impossible to withstand. "You are going to tell me right now how much you need," she said.

"Two hundred and fifty dollars," Ling said quickly.

The American woman opened her purse, counted out the banknotes, thrust them into Ling's hand, and with much eloquence insisted that the girl take the money, pointing out that she had no right to refuse when a child's health was in danger. When Ling permitted herself to be convinced, Patricia insisted she take the car again and deliver the money before they had lunch.

Alone again, Patricia had ordered another gin and was savoring the proud pleasure of having added a good deed to an already considerable list, when she noticed that Helene Jourdain had walked into the bar. Helene, accompanied by a young English officer in uniform, looked embarrassed when their eyes met. Her escort stopped at a distant table, she spoke a few quick words to him, and walked over to Patricia.

"I didn't know you were in Singapore," Patricia said. "I thought you were in one of the hill stations for a few days."

Helene smiled ambiguously. "Oh, Pat, I'm *not* in Singapore."

Patricia glanced at the officer, shrugged her shoulders pityingly, indulgently, and merely murmured, "I see."

She was no longer scandalized by the frivolous behavior of this little French girl. She disapproved of her conduct but forbade herself to pass judgment. The sense of her own superiority permitted her to smile at others' weaknesses, but that was all.

"Just a friend, Pat. Nothing important. . . . Of course, I don't want you to say anything to Robert about seeing me here—it would make trouble. I'm only in town for a few hours."

Patricia assured Helene she could count on her discretion. Ling was back already, crossing the bar toward them. Helene, who was not fond of the Chinese girl, spoke a few more polite words, then left to rejoin her companion. As Ling's eyes followed her, Patricia recalled her friend's request and forewarned the girl. "By the way, Ling, there's no need to say anything about meeting Helene here in Singapore."

"To say anything to whom?" the girl asked, apparently thinking of something else.

"Oh, to . . . to Robert, for example . . . or even to Bernard; it would be best not to mention it at all. It's a woman's business, and has no importance whatever. . . . You will understand such things later on," she added, lowering her eyes, embarrassed by Ling's inquisitive stare.

She changed the subject, and asked her about her family.

"My mother thanks you greatly," said Ling, who had carefully hidden away the money. "She has said the *mem* is too good."

Patricia told her not to mention it, and explained that no one was ever too good. Then she insisted that Ling have a gin with her, which the girl, relieved, happy, and proud of the success of her schemes, accepted.

After a moment, either because of the alcohol's effect or from the simple satisfaction of having brought off a difficult feat, Ling felt a strange sensation. The atmosphere of constraint that usually overpowered her when she was alone with the American woman was gradually disappearing. As she moodily stared at Patricia, her astonishment tempered with admiration in spite of herself, she suddenly felt that a new relationship—a more intimate one, based on a certain mutual esteem—had been established between them. Patricia suspected what had happened, noticing the peculiar quality of her smile, and was delighted. She was sure she would eventually win the girl's heart.

"To your health, my little Ling," she said, lifting her glass.

"To your health, Pat," Ling answered, almost without effort. ". . . Pat?"

"Yes, dear?"

Ling spoke with an intense conviction which, perhaps for the first time, was not inspired by the necessities of the Cause. "You know, Pat, my mother is right. You really are very good—*very, very* good, Pat."

They were lunching at a little table in the hotel grill room. Ling had dropped her peevish reserve and was staring at the people around them, fascinated by the restaurant's bustle that contrasted so strongly with the calm of the bungalow. Whenever her eyes met Patricia's she found herself smiling for no reason whatever.

Patricia congratulated herself on the happy result of this expedition to Singapore, and began thinking up an attractive program for the rest of the afternoon. Her heart was brimming with treasures of wisdom. She agreed with Bernard that she must not put the girl off with too heavy a dose of edification. Certain more cheerful aspects of Western civilization would exert a powerful attraction on any girl her age and contribute to her conversion by making her forget her savage jungle life. She decided that there were many roads leading to the Good. She enjoyed comfort and luxury herself, and often thanked heaven for the lucky coincidence that had accorded the invention of these accessories of well-being to the Christian world.

First she took the girl to the hairdresser she herself visited each week, where Ling had obstinately refused to accompany her until today. It had been difficult enough to persuade the girl to let her hair grow, but she still kept it straight and made no attempt to arrange it becomingly.

In Mr. Chang's beauty parlor, where the fashionable hairdresser also provided other services of a cosmetic nature for his clientele, Ling felt both intimidated and at the same time furious with herself for being affected by the surroundings of this cave, where the most disgusting elements of a rotten society came to conceal their decrepitude. She hated the perfumes, their ridiculous names, and the hideous apparatus required to give a new luster to skins sagging with sloth. But she had yielded to Patricia's whim in a moment of weakness, and now resigned herself to every sacrifice. She sat down in a chair after a second's hesitation and scarcely trembled when Mr. Chang, a Westernized Chinese, touched her hair.

She was rewarded for her docility by feeling only certain endurable pangs—those of curiosity, behind which all her discomfort soon disappeared. This was the effect Patricia had hoped for, watching her out of the corner of her eye from a nearby chair. Ling made a final attempt to push away the drier, then closed her eyes in resignation. She opened them now, dared to look at herself in the mirror, and thought she looked almost funny with this great machine over her head.

"If Kim could see me now," she thought, and the thought amused instead of mortifying her.

Patricia, finished first, stood behind her to consider the effect. She burst out laughing when, after Mr. Chang had removed the drier, Ling made a disappointed grimace. Without even being aware of it, the girl had hoped for something more than this horror. Patricia told her to be patient and advised her to close her eyes again while Mr. Chang set to work with his comb. She herself watched his movements closely, appreciating their effect and occasionally giving advice.

"You can look now."

Ling made an exclamation of happy surprise in spite

of herself. Her delicate face, like that of many Asiatics, was marvelously suited to such Western refinements, and Mr. Chang knew his business. Encouraged by Patricia, he had brought off a masterpiece of his art, of which Patricia was as proud as if it had been a personal success.

"Don't you think you look better this way? To think you never wanted to!"

Ling felt disturbed. She was already reproaching herself for the pleasure she had taken in discovering she was pretty. She looked in the mirror again, frowning. But she could not maintain this savage expression for long, and her features soon relaxed again into a satisfied smile.

"Ling is very pleased," she murmured, bewildered.

"You really are adorable, dear; Bernard won't recognize you tonight."

It was true; Ling was adorable. For a moment she thought about this last remark without quite knowing why, and about the surprise she would cause at the bungalow. Mechanically, she turned back to the mirror. Patricia was paying the cashier, the hairdresser was talking to another customer. Ling quickly patted her hair and caressed a curl. Then she opened her purse, took out the lipstick she rarely used, and delicately applied it to her lips.

In the Eurasian dress shop they visited next, Ling underwent still stranger metamorphoses, alternating rebellion, curiosity, childish satisfaction, and real anguish: at every moment she reproached herself for not being revolted by this frivolity.

"Isn't wonderful?" the Eurasian woman asked, proud of her perfect accent.

Ling, in her underthings, was blushing for shame. Patricia had actually had to look annoyed before she would take off her dress, and each time the dressmaker stared at her, after having draped some stuff around her, the girl held her arms over her breasts in an unconscious gesture of self-defense. But when she felt the contact of the new cloth she could not keep from staring at it greedily.

"Which one do you like best, dear?"

Ling made her choice, after many hesitations. Patricia decided she had good taste; the dressmaker agreed: she had instinctively chosen the most expensive materials.

16   The Singapore ladies were accustomed to gather every afternoon at the swimming club to take tea together under the parasols at the pool's edge. The Singapore ladies stayed there until dark, before meeting again at another club to continue their gossip over the bridge table, drinking many whisky-and-sodas. The Singapore ladies' conversation generally inclined toward certain city scandals, or toward the household problems which the wind of emancipation blowing across Malaya had rendered quite insoluble. Sometimes, however, they tackled more elevated subjects—on occasion, even those of politics.

Patricia was not very fond of the Singapore ladies' society, feeling herself a foreigner among them. Nevertheless, leaving the dressmaker's with still an hour before they were to return home, she decided that Ling might be amused by their chatter and that the animation around the pool might be interesting. The *syce* dropped them at the club before joining the other Malay chauffeurs squatting at the foot of a wall, gossiping together and waiting for their mistresses to call them.

Patricia found the ladies' circle in its usual place, near the diving boards, and headed toward them along the edge of the pool. Ling followed her reluctantly. She had never encountered the Singapore ladies *en masse,* but she loathed the few specimens she had met during their previous visits to Singapore. Nevertheless, the thought of the dollars in her bag mitigated the anguish of the ordeal.

"Next time," Patricia remarked, "we'll try to get here earlier. So as to have time for a swim."

"Oh no, Pat, not here. Not in front of all these people!"

Patricia looked at her with sympathetic curiosity. This kind of modesty on the part of a little savage never failed to fill her with astonishment; but she did not insist. She decided she had won many victories today, and that she must not try to overcome such absurd instincts by force.

They reached the group, which consisted of two French and several English ladies, mostly officials' wives. All stared unkindly at Ling, who turned glum again.

After having greeted Patricia, one of the ladies asked her why they did not see her more often.

"We only come into town once a week, and Bernard wants me back before dark."

"He's quite right. None of the roads are safe now, unfortunately."

This was the point at which the conversation inevitably turned to the terrorists. One of the Frenchwomen declared that they were living in bad times, which announcement was unanimously approved by the Singapore ladies. A judge's wife indignantly told them how she had been unable to find a single Chinese boy to work for her ever since her husband had sentenced a few of the bandits severely, and the rest spent some time commiserating with her on her plight. The servant problem might have distracted their attention and channeled their entire imagination until the end of the session, as it often did. But at that moment a businessman's wife, recently admitted into the circle on account of her bold and original ideas, raised the discussion to its original level by maintaining that the government was responsible for everything, since it refused to take strong measures against these pirates. This remark provoked several timid contradictions, and she went on to say that they would be left in peace if they simply hung two or three hundred Chinese chosen at random and let the rest know about it; that was what she told her husband every day. Ling, who half understood what was being said, drew her features into a forbidding mask and pretended to be interested in the diving boards.

"After all, dear, there are good Chinese too," Patricia objected gently.

This produced no affirmative response. One of the Englishwomen confined herself to saying that she had never suspected the existence of such a thing. As for the other Frenchwoman, it was her husband who had carefully explained the problem to her, and proud of her recent acquisition of knowledge, she remarked that the only way to get rid of the terrorists once and for all was to starve them to death, cutting off all their sources of supply. This proposition was received with unanimous accord, followed by the audacious supposition on the part of the entire circle: "How can they manage to get supplies in the jungle anyway? They must have accomplices everywhere!" At this moment Ling could not keep from smiling cruelly, squeezing her bag down a little harder on her knees.

"And out at Kebun Besar, Pat?" one of the ladies asked. "They say it's quieter there these days."

The question produced an indulgent smile on Patricia's lips and she answered, with a vague, dreamy look, "Yes, it's quiet at Kebun Besar."

"I'd like to know how you manage it."

"That's my secret," Patricia said in the same tone. She was sincerely sorry for them, their eyes so obstinately blindfolded to the truth. All it had taken was a little understanding, a kindly gesture, to restore peace to her world. She looked at Ling tenderly.

"Well, I admire your courage. I'd be dead with fear if I had to live that way—isolated somewhere in a *bungalow.*"

"Fear!" Patricia murmured derisively. "What do you think of that, Ling?"

"Ling is not afraid," the Chinese girl said suddenly in her worst accent, and lifting her head with a fierce expression. "Ling would be afraid to live in Singapore."

These words and their insolent tone produced a frozen silence. The ladies looked at her reproachfully. Then one of them remarked, "Helene Jourdain doesn't agree with you, apparently. She's frightened to death out there. That must be why she comes here so often."

"Singapore has other attractions for her besides being a rest home," another said.

135

The Singapore ladies chuckled, and, having chuckled, pronounced a number of further considerations on Helene's private life and her friends in the city. This lasted until one of the ladies decided to feel sorry for poor Robert, at which point her neighbor judiciously pointed out that Robert had permitted himself a fair amount of compensation.

"Someone saw him at the movies the other night. And do you know with whom? With a Chinese girl—a taxi-girl from the 'Happy World'!"

"I think that's beastly. Helene's perfectly justified in doing anything she wants in Singapore."

Here again the entire chorus indicated its approval. Then the lady with bold ideas, who was also graced with quick wit, remarked that Robert's conduct was certainly reprehensible, but not so bad as that of a certain Eastern industrialist who was always surrounded by Chinese whenever he came to Singapore. This flash was a kind of signal. The chorus received it with new chuckles, and the conversation broke up into a series of private exchanges between neighbor and neighbor, whispered words interrupted by oh's, ah's, and little giggles following sly innuendos. It was the moment of relaxation, of recreation which the Singapore ladies permitted themselves after an elevated discussion whose scope and range could scarcely be sustained too long without fatigue.

Back in the car, Ling huddled in her corner and continued to sulk. This insipid, ill-natured gossiping had reawakened the hatred which the day's distractions had briefly caused her to forget. She clenched her teeth in rage, remembering their remarks.

"Singapore ladies very bad. Ling does not like

them," she answered harshly when Patricia showed concern over her attitude.

Patricia undertook to explain that the girl was taking their pointless chatter a little too seriously. Of course she judged them rather severely herself. She disapproved of their wretched intrigues, their selfishness, and their hard-heartedness; but she found excuses for them in the absurd prejudices of their caste, which condemned them to utter idleness in a country where their only social function was to be waited on. She found a new lesson for her pupil in the incident.

"They are frivolous, but that's not a crime, dear. They didn't really *mean* to hurt your feelings. You must show a little more indulgence of your neighbors. You're not at all tolerant of others. You must learn to forgive human beings their weaknesses. None of us is perfect, unfortunately. I want you to learn how to smile, darling."

Ling looked at her hard. She still had the fleeting impression that some kind of intimacy had been established between them, and she made an effort to preserve it, but her attempt at a smile looked more like a grimace.

Bernard had invited his two assistants home for a drink after a tiring day. The three men were still wearing their shorts, despite the lateness of the hour. They had taken their first drink at teatime, as was frequently the case when the women were away. They were beginning their third. The houseboy had turned on the generator, and the bungalow lights lit up part of the garden.

"I hope Pat won't be late," Bernard murmured. "I don't like her out on the roads at this hour."

"Is she alone?"

"With Ling, of course."

"By the way, what are you going to do with that Chinese girl?" Robert asked, staring at a nightjar that had landed on the lawn.

Ling's presence in the Delavigne's bungalow, if it did not cause a scandal in the district, provoked a good deal of curiosity. She was often discussed, especially by Robert Jourdain and his wife, who lived apart and found in Ling an occasion for an exchange of opinions. Helene was frankly hostile to the girl and violently critical of the equal footing the Delavigne's accorded her. Robert took the opposite point of view, of course, and approved of their attitude. It was purely in a spirit of contradiction that he did so; their relationship had been dictated by this spirit for some time, and fundamentally he was as shocked as Helene by the Delavigne's familiarity.

"The other day Pat told Helene you were going to adopt her. That's a strange idea."

"Why?" Remy objected. "Ling is certainly equal to any European society she might meet." He had shown an interest in the girl for some time now, and always rose to her defense when she was attacked. Bernard hesitated under Robert's gaze, stretched casually, and spoke quite calmly.

"Oh, adopting her! Sometimes Pat has crazy notions like that, and then they pass. . . . After all, Remy, you're quite right—she's nice enough, for a Chinese. . . . She keeps us company—cheers up the bungalow. But that's hardly the same thing as adopting her."

The characteristic sound of the American Ford could be heard as it passed through the plantation. Soon the car came to a stop at the edge of the garden in shadow.

The three men stood up. The houseboy came forward to take the packages. Patricia got out first. Seeing Robert, she leaned toward Ling and murmured to her: "Robert's here, dear. Remember, not a word about Helene."

"Ling has understood," Ling said in a dry tone. While Patricia was giving the boy her packages, Ling walked around the car and approached the veranda, gradually emerging from the darkness. The three men suddenly saw her in full light, and discovered Mr. Chang's masterpiece.

They were astounded at the sight: Ling, elegantly dressed in her city gown, carefully made up, and her hair beautifully groomed, was a spectacle irresistible to Western eyes. Robert gave a low, admiring whistle. Remy said nothing, his mouth open in surprise. Bernard could not resist exclaiming, "Really, Ling!"

The girl turned away, bewildered. Patricia, coming up behind her, forced her to raise her head and show herself. "You mustn't be ashamed, dear," she said, looking at the three men. "Isn't she adorable?"

"Adorable," they repeated simultaneously.

Ling grew a little bolder. Under their appraising looks her features relaxed a little. She blushed with pleasure. Her face gradually brightened. Turning toward Patricia, she finally gave her the frank smile the American woman had asked of her and which she had refused in the car. For a fraction of a second, she was not far from thinking that the cursed universe of the whites had certain agreeable oases.

17   This weakness was once again followed by painful remorse. She felt distressed and wanted to be alone. So as soon as the two assistants had left Ling excused herself, pleading sudden exhaustion, and took refuge in her room. The day had confused her, and she worried about the sense within herself that tended to impose a new vision of the world upon her, a vision insidiously distorted, unreconcilable. . . .

She sat in front of her mirror and looked at her face attentively. She started to make a violent gesture that would undo her hair and destroy Mr. Chang's creation; but her hand hesitated, and her furious movement ended despite herself in a soft caress. She rubbed her lips— though more gently than usual, sometimes stopping absent-mindedly, as if she no longer felt the urgency of the exorcisms she usually performed each evening.

She tried to shake off an importunate preoccupation,

opened her bag, counted out the dollars, and at once felt less nervous. Hearing the sound of Patricia's steps as she was going to bed, Ling cocked her ears, her face still intent. Finally she reacted decisively. She thrust the money into her pocket, made a face as if she were spitting toward her benefactress' room, and snarled her usual abuse, but this time with an accent whose conviction seemed the fruit of a long internal debate. "Pigs!"

When she met Kim a little later at the edge of the jungle, she rushed toward him without taking the usual precautions, enjoying his surprise in advance.

"Kim! Oh, Kim, I have the dollars!"

"My little sister Ling works miracles!" the terrorist cried. "How did you get them?"

Ling explained that she had sold a present from the American *mem*. Then the American *mem*, again, had given her the rest for her family.

"But my family is not good," she said bitterly. "My mother is an old backward woman without dignity. Ling has kept the money for the comrades. Kim can buy the machine guns."

"Thank you, little sister," he breathed fervently. Then, after a moment's thought, he said with intense conviction, "Our great leader Ho was right. I was wrong to doubt. It is heaven who has placed the American woman in our path."

"It is heaven," Ling agreed, relapsing into her reverie.

This trip to Singapore marked the beginning of a slow metamorphosis for Ling. In the course of the months that followed, her appearance modified as much as her social deportment. Her manner became more natural. Gradually she lost her tense bearing, the harsh grimace that always produced a certain uneasiness when she was with Europeans. She learned how to speak French and English correctly. The Europeans of the district grew accustomed to consider her as one of their number and were not embarrassed to carry on in her hearing conversations of the most naïve egoism, betraying their frank sense of racial superiority to all Asiatic peoples. She no longer bridled when she heard such remarks; she seemed a part of their world. She even listened to the Singapore ladies without impatience.

She walked, she dressed, she ate, she laughed, she sat in a chair like all the white women in Malaya. When they waited on her at the club or in a Singapore restaurant, the Chinese boys themselves forgot that she was one of them. Rawlinson, who had followed the progress of this transformation with growing interest, often looked at her wonderingly. He had never tried to resolve the vague doubt that occasionally still troubled him as to her background. If a professional scruple disturbed him, it was enough merely to look at Ling to be reassured. This girl who played tennis, who obviously enjoyed being elegant, and who danced with so much zest, could not be a terrorist. His whole experience of criminals and outlaws forbade any such suspicion.

So he warmly congratulated Patricia on her surprising success. Not only, he told her, had she snatched the girl from a miserable life—and probably from prostitution as well, since that was the usual fate of girls of her class in Singapore—but she had actually managed to make her into a woman of the world. "And of the best world at that—ours," he added in the toneless voice he always used.

Patricia smiled at these compliments, and her satisfaction increased when she decided that Ling's physical metamorphosis was a minor thing compared to the spiritual evolution she perceived in the girl.

And on this point, as on so many others, perhaps Patricia was right. Perhaps Ling's savage instincts were in the process of becoming milder without her knowing it, merely from accompanying her guide so often along the paths of righteousness, from submitting every day to the stubborn assaults that Patricia's affectionate tenderness and her inexorable solicitude made upon her.

PART FOUR

18   The powers of Good are indeed invincible, as Ling was discovering to her confusion. The powers of Good are irresistible. Human nature is so compacted of noble, generous, charitable sentiments that even if many of these sentiments are momentarily in eclipse, indiscernible, the Good always manages to discover in that nature some element ready to enter into composition with itself. And as soon as the weak point is determined, the powers of Good focus and multiply their assaults without leaving the crippled soul a moment's respite.

In behalf of Ling's salvation, the powers of Good had found in Patricia a minister possessing to a rare degree both faith and skill. The continual affection with which the American woman treated the girl, her gentleness, her indulgence, her inexhaustible charity, the kindness of which she herself was a sterling example, constituted arms more effective in the service of Good, more subtle and more formidable than the most refined tortures. Ling felt as if she was being plunged at each moment into an ingenious bath of elixirs whose perfumes were overpowering her while the chemistry of the insidious essences tended to dissolve the rebellion in her spirit. If she still managed to revolt inwardly against Christian morality at the very moment she was being subjected to its lessons, it was with a growing frequency that she allowed herself afterward to reflect upon the seductive nobility of its precepts.

Every day unaccustomed ideas, feelings, images alien until this moment, appeared in her mind: she was beginning to discover that the people around her were *nice*. This word, hitherto despised, and the repugnant attitude it expressed affected her: she was beginning to appreciate its perfidious sweetness.

This evening she returned to her room, her arms full of presents given her to celebrate her twentieth birthday, confused by the wine she had drunk and dazzled by the compliments she had received during the dinner in honor of the occasion.

The entire white personnel of Kebun Besar had been invited. First Patricia had kissed her, then Bernard, paternally; then Helene—Ling knew the Frenchwoman did not like her, but her parrot's pretense of amiability was beginning to amuse her. Finally, laughing and joking, Robert and Remy had kissed her in their turn. And such ridiculous behavior had not shocked her. On the contrary, they were all nice, implacably nice! Especially Remy, who was giving evidence of a growing interest in her, and who behaved so strangely in her company. The other day, after a game of tennis, he had seized her hand and held it in his own. At the time she had not found this disagreeable. It was only after forcing herself to think about it that she had recoiled.

That was what she needed to do—think—but this operation was costing an increasingly painful effort. Today she had decided to hold a serious session of self-criticism. No sooner had she pushed open her door than she was distracted from her project by the packages she was carrying.

She opened the boxes and looked at her presents again: an evening dress and a pearl necklace. The dress was from Patricia. The necklace was to replace the one she said she had lost; it was from Bernard. It was much more beautiful than the other. Examining its luster when she had first received it, she had felt a sudden bitter twinge and a strange desire to cry. And she had thrown herself into his arms with an instinctive gesture of affection. He was nice, too. And with Ling Bernard found himself abandoning his brusque manner. He seemed touched by her spontaneity and had mechanically caressed her hair . . . caressed her as if she were a puppy! . . . She absolutely had to have her self-criticism session.

She busied herself in an effort to gather together the peculiar and contradictory elements of her conscience, the better to set them in order, to become more methodically aware of herself: it was the periodic undertaking of all the greatest human minds, the most extravagant of all the spirit's operations, doomed from the start by its very nature to a total and tragic failure. She succeeded no better than the profoundest philosophers in hunting the shadows from her soul, and no worse: there are no degrees in matters of absolute impossibility. After a long effort, she finally gave up, exasperated, her mind routed.

The guests had gone; Bernard and Patricia were in bed; the bungalow and its surroundings, utterly silent. It was the night of her weekly task. Kim was waiting for her at the edge of the jungle—Kim, with whom she had exchanged vows. She had not yet prepared her bundle.

The chest was there, brought in by the houseboy with the two suitcases for the orphans and her own family. She began her clandestine selection as usual, setting aside the comrades' share. The task had become, by now, a routine chore.

Suddenly, at the moment she was putting aside the chocolate bars that were so precious to the terrorists, the image of a sickly orphan rose before her eyes, the boy she had so despised for his servility. But far from making her angry this time, the vision upset her deeply. She had never before experienced such a sensation, and she did not dare account for it to herself. Her whole body trembled as if she had caught some subtle disease, and in the voluptuousness of this fever she vaguely divined an unspecified and terrible danger.

She made a sound, an exclamation of furious distress, realizing that she had yielded, unconsciously, to the powers of Good. An angel of temptation had impelled her to return the chocolate to the orphans' stock. Quickly, in order to escape the spell, she threw the whole package into Kim's bundle. Then she rushed toward the chair where she had piled her birthday presents. She seized the dress between rigid fingers, thrust her fist toward her benefactors' bedrooms, and in a desperate voice, with a last pathetic effort to reanimate a failing conviction, screamed, "Pigs! Pigs!"

19   Patricia, who was lovingly cultivating the flowers in her garden, straightened up from her bent-over position and felt a slight ache in her hips. She remembered how soon she was going to be forty-five; though she had managed, thank God, to hold on to her figure and her suppleness, certain efforts caused her more fatigue than they used to. She smiled instead of frowning. She could grow old now. Her foster daughter—she was still insisting on adopting Ling; the formal arrangements would be made during Bernard's forthcoming leave in France—her foster daughter would be Patricia's second youth. Her life had assumed a profound meaning since she had devoted herself to the Chinese girl's reformation and education, and observing Ling's progress kept Patricia in a state of permanent euphoria.

She glanced toward the silent bungalow. The boy was dusting the furniture with an almost immaterial feather duster. Bernard was probably still asleep; for some time now he had permitted himself to stay in bed on Sunday mornings. She smiled, thinking how well her husband's character had developed during these last months. His attitude toward the natives had become more humane. Ling was kindling a light to which Bernard, too, was responding.

Ling was not there this morning: Remy had called for her early to take her to the tennis courts. Patricia gazed at the lawn, where the bustle contrasted with the bungalow's drowsiness.

"At last," she murmured, "it's beginning to look like a garden!" This progress was the result of an increase in manpower and a utilization of all the available skills. Outraged at seeing the inactive *mata-matas* maintaining a day-long fictive guard against a chimerical enemy, Patricia had transformed them all into gardeners. At the moment they were working behind her, digging new beds. Bernard had protested at first but eventually had submitted with philosophical calm. The district was perfectly calm now. The terrorists seemed a bad dream. Kebun Besar was an oasis of peace in a troubled Malaya.

Bernard came out of the bathroom, still dressing. As he crossed the living room he spoke to the houseboy in a jovial tone. "How are you feeling, boy?"

"Very well, *Tuan.*"

As soon as his back was turned, the boy stopped working to stare after him with worried eyes. It had been difficult enough not to hear him shout when he spoke, but to have the *Tuan* ask after his health! . . . He felt as if the universal order had been overturned and anticipated nothing good from this unsuspected development.

Bernard, after happily kissing Patricia, looked around him and his face brightened still further. The morning was radiant. The garden blazed with a thousand colors. He decided it had been a good idea to have the rest of the barbed wire cleared away. He leaned over a flower, inhaled its fragrance, and complimented his wife.

"What do you think of my gardeners?" she asked, pointing to the half-naked *mata-matas* busily working behind them.

Bernard admitted that they were in their element at last. These boys, abruptly recruited from the *kampongs,* were about as suitable for wearing a uniform as he was for saying mass. He joked with them in Malay. They burst out laughing. Patricia watched them with satisfaction.

"You've changed too, dear."

He did not attempt to deny it and embraced her again with adolescent enthusiasm. "Thanks to you, darling. . . . Pat, Pat, you're a witch."

He walked around the garden with her, then looked at his watch and walked over to his car. "I'm going to the office." He hesitated a moment, as if he had suddenly had an idea. "I'll probably go out to the club before I come home. I'll drive Ling back."

Patricia thought she might come with him. He dissuaded her, pointing out that he would have to be at his office for some time first.

"All right," she said, "but don't work too hard. Don't forget, today's a day of rest."

"I'm not forgetting," Bernard assured her warmly.

About to get into the car, he changed his mind, turned to have a last look at the garden and the Malays, and then kissed Patricia passionately. "No, not a witch, Pat, a good fairy! . . . You've waved your magic wand and the two worst pests in the country have disappeared: the terrorists and the police."

Her hair tousled, Patricia indulgently shrugged her shoulders and looked after the car as it disappeared under the trees, then bent once more over her flowers.

"*Mem?*"

The boy had stopped working and approached her in silence. He was standing behind her, frowning, his eyes on the ground, with that severe look some Asiatic faces assume to express a profound dissatisfaction.

"What is it?"

"Boy wish to speak to *mem*. Speak serious."

"Speak. You look serious already."

"*Missi* leave at night," the boy said, after a moment of silence during which he would not look at her.

"What?"

"*Missi* leave at night."

Patricia's face darkened suddenly, even before she had determined the full importance of this information. The garden looked darker to her. The boy began talking very fast, still avoiding her eyes.

"*Missi* leave at night to meet comrades. Every week. Boy heard and watched for long time. *Missi* carry big package. Boy thought: very bad! Tried to follow. Hard to do. *Missi* walk very fast; no more noise than cobra. Only last week, boy able to do. *Missi* go near jungle and stop. Boy watched, lying on ground. Man left jungle; bad man; terrorist with red star in cap and machine gun. When man come near, *Missi* give package and letter. *Missi* say to take as usual like presents for children."

"Oh dear!" breathed Patricia, bringing her hand to her heart.

"*Missi* say to come back next Friday," the Chinese continued. "Boy not like. Think: very bad. Speak to *mem*."

"Listen to me . . ." Patricia said. She tried to control herself after her first astonishment. As much to reassure herself as to put off the boy, she decided that Ling could not have given evidence of such duplicity for so long a time. "Listen to me. You have done well, but from now on you will not spy on *Missi*. And above all you will speak to no one about this, not even to the *Tuan*, do you understand? I will look into it myself. . . . There is certainly some very simple and very innocent explanation. Do you understand?"

"Yes, *mem*," the boy said. He went back into the house, shaking his head, more convinced than ever that things would turn out badly.

20   Bernard felt lighthearted at the wheel.
He thought he saw a strange light in the pale Malay sky,
a brightness that awakened forgotten feelings within
him. He began to hum, driving rather carelessly. When
two roe deer sprang up in front of the car he pressed
the accelerator to catch up with them. When they left
the road and disappeared among the trees, he let go
of the wheel, moved his arms as if he were shouldering
an imaginary rifle, and returned the car to the road just
as it was going over the shoulder.

He parked in front of the office. The grounds were
deserted, and he admired the green plants he had had
the *mata-matas* put in the day before; here, too, the gar-
rison had been transformed into gardeners. "That's
much more cheerful," he murmured. "These Malays
have taste."

The main room was open. The clerks did not work on Sunday, but Mr. Gopal was there alone, putting his accounts in order.

"Good morning, sir," he said as he stood up.

"Good morning." Suddenly Bernard felt an enormous compassion for this old man nailed to his desk, on a plantation lost in the middle of the jungle. Robert Jourdain's arrival distracted him momentarily from the reflections which this spectacle had inspired. He responded absent-mindedly to his assistant's greeting. "Hello, Robert . . . just a minute, I'll be with you. . . . Mr. Gopal," he continued in a tone of affectionate reproach, "do you really have to spend every Sunday morning over our books? Haven't you any grandchildren," he went on in a livelier tone, "someone who would like to play with you in your garden?"

"Sir . . ." stammered the astonished Mr. Gopal, ". . . the accounts . . ."

"Leave them for tomorrow," Bernard said decisively, "and go spend the day with your family."

"Very well, sir." The clerk hesitated another moment, as if to convince himself he had really heard the words; but there was no possible doubt. He arranged his books in a neat pile and prepared to leave the office. Bernard further increased his stupefaction by sending his regards to Mr. Gopal's wife.

Robert Jourdain had watched this scene inattentively enough, but Bernard felt vaguely embarrassed, and it occurred to him that so unaccustomed an attitude on his part required some explanation.

"It's true after all," he said sharply, as if replying to a contradiction, "these people are men like ourselves, Robert. They have families, souls. We treat them too much like tools. We ought to have more consideration for them—for their inner lives. . . . Don't you think so?"

Robert agreed with him, but coldly, and Bernard thought he detected a mocking intonation in his voice. Then Robert reminded him of the reason for his visit. He had come to call for Bernard, as had been decided the day before, to visit part of the plantation where the rubber trees were suffering from a strange epidemic. Bernard, who had forgotten the appointment, looked annoyed and said he would not go, mentioning the office work that was waiting for him. He had enough for two hours.

"And afterwards Pat asked me to stop by the club to pick up Ling."

"Ling is at the club?"

"Yes, playing tennis with Remy. . . . So will you go look at the trees without me and do the best you can?"

Robert left him, heading toward the interior of the plantation. Bernard, watching from the window, heaved a sigh of relief when he disappeared.

He left the building, jumped into his car, and drove off in the opposite direction. As he passed Mr. Gopal's bungalow he noticed the latter in a sarong, strolling with his family. They all bowed very low to him. He felt gratified, and promised himself he would add to the patch of land he had given the old clerk for gardening.

The club boy had changed into his Sunday uniform. Although there were no members at the bar he stood at his post behind it, facing the tennis court where Ling and Remy were finishing a set. He watched the girl's movements through his narrowed eyes, and no one in the world could have imagined the nature of his reflections. The rest of the club was empty. The planters rarely came there on Sunday morning. Some were working; the rest preferred to enjoy their day of rest more intensely by napping in an armchair on their bungalow verandas.

"Your game, Ling," said Remy, coming up to the net. "You're doing very well. . . . Another set?"

"In a minute. I'm tired."

She sat down on a bench at the edge of the court. The boy interrupted his solitary meditation, prepared his tray, and waited for them to call him.

"I'm glad to be with you this morning," said Remy as he sat down beside her.

"Me too. I love tennis." She smiled. For some time now her smile had changed. It was a white woman's smile. She had become conscious of her weapons, and it was obvious that the young man's confusion did not displease her.

"Especially since it's the only chance I have to see you alone. You're really doing awfully well."

"So you said."

"I mean . . . your general progress, Ling."

"Yes."

He put his hand over hers. She did not pull it away, and looked at him for a moment, inquisitively. She found these games amusing. Moreover, she was impressed by the charm and amiability of the people around her. She felt increasingly reluctant to cause her fellow creatures the least discomfort by rejecting their affection. Remy drew closer. He had already kissed her . . . he had kissed her and she hadn't slapped him! As she was about to, her courage had failed her. He was so nice! But this time she slipped away with a little laugh and stood up. "The boy is watching us, and I want to improve my game."

At the bar, the boy watched them return to the court, abandoned his tray, and resumed his reverie. He broke off quickly, his ear cocked, as he heard the hum of a motor. He could not be mistaken: he knew every one of the planters' cars by sound. It was *Tuan* Delavigne's car driving in at the club. He assumed the respectful look suitable for receiving a senior manager and made ready to wait on him. But Bernard quickly walked past the bar and approached the two young people.

"Good morning, children. Nice day . . . I'll take you home, Ling," he continued in a casual tone of voice.

"Already? I'd have taken her back." Remy barely concealed his disappointment.

Bernard explained lightly that Pat had asked them to be home early.

"I'll go and change; I'll be back in a minute," Ling said and disappeared into the dressing rooms. Bernard invited Remy to have a drink. The boy began to shake up a cocktail while Bernard walked up and down in front of the bar, whistling to regain his composure.

The Chinese suddenly stopped, his hands in the air. Another car was approaching: *Tuan* Jourdain's, he was sure. That the three White Men of Kebun Besar should have arrived at the club in different vehicles at different intervals seemed to him a shocking anomaly. He stood stock-still for a second before resuming his work and his impassivity.

It was Robert Jourdain, and his glance at Bernard's car parked under the portico betrayed his embarrassment and his bad humor.

"I thought you were going to see those sick trees," Bernard said sullenly.

Robert mumbled that it had been too hot, that he had suddenly wanted something cool to drink. "And what about you? I thought you had so much work at the office."

Bernard reluctantly explained that his wife had telephoned him to bring Ling home early. All three men drank in silence. Bernard's irritation disappeared only when Ling returned, absolutely ravishing, he thought, in her white skirt, with her racket under her arm. All his enthusiasm restored, he hastened their departure without making any excuses for it, jovially clapping his young assistant on the shoulder. "There she is! *Au revoir,* old boy! Forgive me for depriving you of your partner. So long Robert. Coming, Ling?"

21   "You're not annoyed with me for breaking up your match?"

He glanced at her out of the corner of his eye while he was driving, concerned at the thought that he might have caused her the slightest irritation. He felt almost timid. It was a rather strange feeling for a man his age, and he did not know if he should be glad about it or mortified. He had said nothing since they had left the club. Ling answered gaily that she wasn't annoyed in the slightest.

"Since Pat needs me . . ."

"To tell the truth, Ling, I . . ." He stammered like a truant schoolboy. She turned toward him and noticed his embarrassment. Coming from Bernard, such behavior seemed somehow agreeable, and to put him at his ease she smiled at him broadly.

"Yes?"

He hesitated again, then changed his manner and spoke jovially, as he had with Remy a while before. "Oh, well, you know, I suddenly realized that it was Sunday, that it was a beautiful day, and that there were so many interesting things to see around here . . ."

It was true. He hadn't thought anything else. He had merely felt an unaccustomed enthusiasm. He stopped the car abruptly before they reached the plantation gate, at the point where a path crossed the road into the jungle.

Seized by a sudden idea, he put his hand on her shoulder. "Ling, we almost never leave the plantation. Suppose we drive as far as the Malay *kampong* on the river? It's not far, and I haven't set foot there in years."

Ling clapped her hands in genuine enthusiasm. The idea delighted her as much as it did Bernard. For some time she had been feeling a strange curiosity about the outside world, formerly disdained. Happy to discover the same impulse in her benefactor, she moved a little closer to him with a gesture of friendly confidence that he found positively touching.

"What a lovely idea, Bernard! I've never been there."

Her way of calling him by his first name, as she did Pat, was quite natural now. The car turned onto the ragged road that soon became a path half choked with jungle weeds. They got out and continued on foot. To help her over a difficult spot, he put his arm around her shoulders and unconsciously left it there afterwards. She yielded to his authority, taking pleasure in his support and in listening to the warnings he lavished upon her as if she were a child.

The village was not far. They soon came out into the clearing that was its site on the river bank. It was a typical *kampong*, where a few Malays made a living fishing, hunting, and growing a little rice in the surrounding paddy. There were no more than five or six houses, all in the same style: painted wood stakes covered with a roof of attap leaves in the form of a Moslem crescent. Around the buildings, under the gentle shade of the coconut palms, a troop of half-naked children played. On the river a fisherman standing up in his boat was about to cast his net. A little farther away a group of girls Ling's age were bathing, dressed in the Malay fashion, their sarongs wrapped around them and knotted over their breasts.

There were hundreds of such well-hidden places all over Malaya, but to Bernard this one seemed of unsuspected beauty. His sense of it was so thrilling that he felt a strange desire to weep. Instinctively he looked at his companion and was ravished to discover, reflected in her eyes, the image of his own emotion.

A water buffalo sprawling in the mud raised its suspicious head toward them. They had been seen. Breaking off their games, the children rushed toward them, laughing and nudging each other. The girls waved their arms in greeting. Two boys were already shinnying up the palms, sending down a rain of the golden nuts. An old man sitting on a bench, silently contemplating the river, stood up, greeted them with dignity, and wished them welcome. Soon they were offered a profusion of fruits.

They left the *kampong* regretfully, after having laughed and joked with the natives. As they were turning back down the jungle path, accompanied by a procession of children, Bernard again put his protecting arm around Ling's shoulders and let his happiness speak out. "When I think that all this exists two steps away from our door, Ling! Only we never come this way!" After a moment's thought he added sententiously, "And we're very wrong. These people have a soul, their world is just as interesting as ours. Pat tells me so every other minute. . . . Are you happy, Ling?"

She assured him she was delighted; and the pleasure shining in her eyes was certainly real. All Patricia's lessons had left their mark. Ling no longer lived so much to herself, in the savage adoration of an abstract cause; she was becoming a human being. Her heart was opening to the seduction of forms and images. At this moment, she did not have the courage to despise the Malays' docility; she even felt something like affection for their carefree happiness.

They climbed back into the car and returned to the road. After a long silence Bernard remarked casually, "Of course, Ling, there's no need to tell anyone we were here . . . the two of us."

She looked at him, surprised, perhaps, but not at all shocked. The perfume of mystery that was beginning to impregnate their escapade quite naturally allied itself with the subtle aromas that wafted through her new universe.

"Tell whom?"

She had asked the question ingenuously enough, but there was an unfamiliar tone in her voice: a trace of irony, a suspicion of weariness, and a dawning confusion; a mixture of anxiety and pleasure at the obscure presentiment of being confronted once more by an assault, from an unsuspected direction, of the irresistible powers of Good.

". . . Why, Pat, of course. I told her I would be staying at the office to work. . . . You understand me, don't you?"

"Ling has understood," she declared, resuming her old way of expressing herself, but with the new smile that reflected the spirit of her recent development.

He slowed the car in order to look at her more closely. His own smile and his voice betrayed his delighted admiration when he murmured to her, as Remy had an hour before, "My little Ling . . . you're really doing awfully well!"

They returned, unhurriedly, by a route that Bernard capriciously enjoyed prolonging. He decided to take a lane that followed the boundaries of the entire plantation. He could not bring himself to cut this excursion short.

They stopped at the Tamil village where once before, at dawn, he had pitilessly pursued the malingering workers. From a distance the village had the formality and the geometrical precision of a workers' project, with its identical iron-roofed houses symmetrically lined up.

"It's not as pretty as the Malay *kampong*," Ling remarked, making a face.

He agreed, with something like nostalgia. "It's a village we made. . . . Nevertheless," he added suddenly, "when you get close to it it looks quite different. Come and see."

He led her on again, eager to share in her discovery of a new Malaya, his own sense of it dawning with the furtive impressions he was scarcely aware of registering. He was delighted to notice, as they approached, that his intuition had not deceived him. The dreamed-of world rose out of a thousand trivial details, like those gods with animal heads he passed every day without seeing them, and which, this morning, assumed for him the affecting colors and proportions of poetry itself.

They reached the very heart of the village, and his enchantment grew at the complete realization of his promise made to Ling on the faith of his confused recollections. It was true: close to, the village lost its workers'-project look entirely, each of its inhabitants having created around himself the picturesque climate of his country. It produced a delirious impression on Bernard. At that moment, in this dirty village, he was steeped in all the exoticism of the East.

It was the hour of the midday nap. In the square of stamped earth that constituted a kitchen, between the concrete pillars, reigned the exuberant din and the healthy dirt of the Indies which used to drive him beside himself with rage. The women, dressed in red saris, their arms bare, were stirring great pots of rice, like witches over their black cauldrons. Around them a swarm of naked children, demons with long, braided hair, disputed the terrain with all kinds of animals: dogs, yellow sheep with red eyes, emaciated chickens, pigs, cows that spread their sacred dung in every direction.

The racket died away as soon as Bernard appeared, and it was with a certain regret that he felt weighing upon him the anxiety of so many worried looks. An old man—the same one he had fined—looked at his cow that was dirtying the kitchen and slowly approached the creature to lead it away.

"Leave her alone," Bernard said in Tamil.

The old man stopped, abashed by these words and

by the smile that accompanied them. He began to whisper with his neighbors, and their murmur spread to all the houses. It was reported that the master was in a good humor, and the normal village uproar gradually resumed.

The wild demons approached, timidly at first, then with increasing boldness. Ling found herself examining them with interest and indulgence. One baby was lying near her in a hammock improvised from a sarong stretched between two posts. The child was evidently sick, and a woman explained in Tamil that it had had the fever for two days. Bernard translated. Then Ling made an instinctive gesture—a strange one for her, of which she was ashamed a moment later. She approached the hammock, with a maternal gesture chased away the flies that were pestering the child, and wiped the sweat covering its forehead with her own handkerchief.

They explored the village, followed by the utterly subjugated demons, greeted by warmer and warmer salaams. Bernard leaned over a cauldron, took out a handful of rice, dipped it in two or three sauces, and tasted it. "Not bad," he said with the air of a gourmet, "but not quite strong enough. It needs peppers."

At this point the enthusiasm the Tamils had begun to show at his new behavior rose a number of degrees, and several cheers were heard. Gesticulating to indicate his feelings more generally, one man spread out a huge banana leaf on the ground, mixed several handfuls of rice and various other ingredients upon it, and implored them to try his concoction, which was the best in the village. They tasted it, laughing as they licked their fingers.

Suddenly Bernard realized it was late. They tore

themselves away from the delights of this improvised feast and left, accompanied by a delirious crowd. There were tears in Bernard's eyes.

"I never would have guessed they were so sensitive, Ling. Pat is absolutely right: a friendly gesture is enough to gain their devotion. . . . That's how Malaya is," he continued vehemently. "The free and easy life of the Malays themselves, the spices of the Indies . . ."

"There are the Chinese, too," Ling said with a smile.

She pointed to a shop run by a Celestial merchant who sold his wares to the coolies. The man was sitting in front of the shop with his whole family and greeted them with a smile.

"There are the Chinese too," Bernard repeated musingly. This remark seemed to plunge him into a deep meditation. The car was heading toward the bungalow now. All around them was nothing but the silence of the plantation asleep in the sun. Bernard slowed down. "There are the Chinese too," he murmured again, amazement in his voice.

Without stopping the car, he put his arm around her shoulders with the same fatherly gesture he had made several times during the day, but with a warmer solicitude. At the same moment he cried out triumphantly, as if all at once he was dazzled by the luminous evidence of a sensational discovery: "Oh Ling, Ling, how right Pat is! We must win the Asiatic heart with love!"

22   As soon as she saw Kim on the path at the edge of the jungle, Ling rushed toward him without waiting for the signal to be repeated.

"Kim! Oh, Kim, take me away! I beg you to—I can't stay here any more."

He was uncertain of the meaning of this outburst. "Are they suspicious of you?"

"It's not that."

"Is there something new?"

"No . . . always the same thing," she said, lowering her head. "They're always caressing me."

Kim trembled at the thought of the moral sufferings Ling was having to endure in the rotten world of the whites, but today he had no right to display his feelings. He repressed a movement of sympathy and continued in a serious tone. "Patience, little sister. It may be you will come back to us soon."

"Soon!" Her exclamation had a strange note—an anguish he attributed to her burning desire to escape from that inferno.

"Perhaps. First you must perform one more service for our cause."

Then Ling noticed his disturbed expression and asked for the latest news. He told her that Ho had been taken prisoner by the English police. The terrorist general staff was trying to get him back at any cost. He was an indispensable leader. It had been decided to exchange him, but they needed an important hostage, and taking a living European captive was difficult. Every partisan camp in Malaya had been alerted. Kim had thought of kidnaping the manager of Kebun Besar. There were a number of arguments favoring such a plan: the plantation had been left in peace for a long time, and according to Ling's reports the personnel was off guard. "He always goes out with his machine gun just the same," Ling interrupted quickly. "And he's brave."

"I know it. That's exactly why Ling can play a decisive part. It is Ling who will decide if the operation should be attempted."

He explained to her that he had received very strict orders. The attack must not be executed unless success was certain, for fear of alerting the other districts. They needed an important hostage, not a corpse.

He took a charge of machine-gun ammunition out of his pocket and gave it to Ling.

"This looks like regular ammunition, but it's only blanks. If you can put it in the French planter's gun without his noticing the change, we shall have no trouble taking him. Then you will return to us. Do you think you can do that?"

Ling examined the charge. She knew what to do with guns. "I will try," she said in a low voice. "When?"

"Tomorrow. You have told me you are all to spend the evening in Singapore?"

Ling trembled. It was an excursion planned long before, one in which the whole staff was to participate: an occasion Patricia had created to permit Ling to wear her evening gown. The official pretext was the celebration of their leave, which was to take place in a month.

"Tomorrow!"

"Tomorrow. You will certainly return very late at night, and the Frenchman will have drunk heavily, like all the whites when they go into the city. When you return he will sleep deeply. If Ling has been able to make his weapon harmless, he will be at our mercy. Now, listen carefully . . ."

He gave her his last instructions. Ling stammered that she would do her best. Leaving her a few moments later, Kim noticed her distress and again pitied her lot. "Courage, little sister, perhaps it is the last test. The Party will remember what you have suffered for the Cause."

Patricia, who was not yet asleep, had heard the slight sound Ling made opening her window. She got up noiselessly, knocked at the girl's door, received no answer, and tried to open it. As usual, Ling had locked it from inside. Silently, Patricia left the bungalow, walked around the garden to the girl's window, and discovered she was not in her room.

"Dear, it was true," she murmured sadly.

She stepped through the window into the room where she waited in the darkness, from time to time sipping a glass of whisky she had taken out of the kitchen and bitterly reproaching herself: she should have realized that Ling's past could not be wiped out with a feather duster. She had been tempted—threatened, perhaps, by her former comrades. She certainly had excuses. "It's important," she thought, "that Bernard should know nothing about it." If he learned the truth he would find it all too easy to reprove her for her absurd charity and to resume his former attitude. He would surely send Ling away, and all her work would have been for nothing. She could not admit such a painful failure. A furtive step outside made her tremble. She flattened herself into the chair. Ling stepped over the railing, crossed the room in darkness, and turned on the light. Before she even noticed her, Patricia could see the girl's bewildered look and felt touched by it. Obviously her present conduct was hurting her. Patricia regained her confidence in the outcome of her intervention.

"Pat!"

A reflex precipitated Ling toward the window. Patricia stood in her path, a finger on her lips. "Shhh! You'll wake Bernard. Sit down."

Ling collapsed in a chair. Patricia gave her a drink. "Running around all night," she said in a tone of gentle reproach. "What ideas you have, dear! Where have you been?" she asked with authority.

"Seeing a comrade," the Chinese girl answered, her teeth clenched, her head high.

"I knew it. One of your former . . . comrades?"

Ling nodded. She gradually recovered control of herself. The fact of being unmasked and the necessity of confronting an adversary restored her cool-headedness. At last she would be subjected to reproaches, and be able to reply with insults of hatred and scorn. "I take them food and supplies every week, Pat. . . . Whatever I can steal here," she continued insolently.

"Whatever you can take from what is meant for the poor," the American woman said calmly. "Why do you do that, Ling?"

Ling looked at her, terribly disappointed. Patricia was speaking without anger, in a tone of pained melancholy. Ling forced herself to maintain an attitude of defiance for a moment more, then lowered her head, worsted, in despair of finding in this good will and this massive calm a vulnerable point in which to sink her claws.

"Why do you do that?" Patricia repeated. "You can tell me—I am your friend." She was looking at Ling with an imploring expression. She almost seemed to be pleading for a show of affection. "A *comrade*," she continued slowly. "That's what I'm trying to be for you. I don't know if you've noticed it, dear, but I feel so lonely here. . . . I am an American, Ling."

Confronted with the visible anguish of her expression, with the disappointment that was its cause, Ling felt the contagion of pity spreading within her new self and suffered remorse.

"I am an American, Ling," Patricia continued nostalgically. "Of course the Englishwomen will not be my friends. You understand me?"

"I understand," Ling stammered, moved despite herself.

". . . And the French are so different. . . . Ling,

Ling," she went on in agitation, "don't you have a custom—a practice—among your people, your comrades, of confessing your sins to one another? Can't you tell the truth to your friend? Why did you do that?"

Ling felt herself dissolving in the honey of this ingenuous and intractable tenderness. Bewildered, her claws clipped again, increasingly conscious of having sinned, she found herself speaking quite naturally in Patricia's manner, uncertain whether she was sincere or if an ardent desire to console her benefactress had induced a hypocritical confession. She murmured pityingly, "I shared their life for so long, Pat! It's a hard life, you cannot imagine it . . . a life full of suffering and danger."

In spite of her confusion, she noticed, from under her lowered lids, that Patricia seemed to be touched, and continued with greater assurance. "I know they are often sick . . . that sometimes they die because there is no medicine and no care for them. Sometimes, Pat, there is nothing to eat but roots."

"Dear," cried Pat, her voice changing, "has it gone that far?"

Ling's words had the effect of a revelation upon her, and she felt a sudden shame at not having discovered sooner the apparent reason for the girl's behavior. Ling continued in the same melancholy tone which Pat did not recognize as her own.

"It's much worse, Pat. . . . And here, you know, I have everything I want, thanks to you. I live in luxury. I was ashamed of myself. I thought it was my duty to help them. And that's why," she concluded, hanging her head still lower.

At these words, Patricia, quite overcome, seized her hands impetuously, and in a heartfelt cry gave vent to her passionate charity as well as to her relief: "But those are wonderful feelings, my little Ling! Darling, I'm so happy, and so guilty to have doubted you! I should have been wiser. It's a duty to help the wretched. Only . . . only," she added, more calmly, "why deprive the orphans? You should have had more confidence in me. You should have asked me . . ."

And Ling, her eyes wide with astonishment, found only strength to stammer, "Ask you, Pat . . . ask you?"

"Of course," the American woman cried, as if she were producing her triumphant evidence. "Whom else should you ask? Dear, dear," she went on agitatedly, "I won't sleep tonight thinking of those poor men suffering from hunger, exposed to all the dangers of the jungle. . . . I don't suppose they even have mosquito netting . . ."

"No mosquito netting, Pat," Ling murmured sadly, "no sheets, no beds most of the time."

Pat interrupted her decisively. It was not in her energetic nature to lose time in sterile regrets. "Ling, you know what we'll do? Next week we'll make up a bundle together. . . . Let's see, what do they need most?"

The woman of action was never far from the almsgiver in Patricia. Her practical sense, in the service of an insatiable vocation, was already sketching a plan of battle for bringing aid to the miseries of humanity, attentive to what was most urgent and most likely to be effective. "Tell me, Ling, in order of need," she said.

Ling was under the yoke. She took out of her pocket a paper covered with Chinese characters and began to read it aloud. It was the list Kim gave her each week.

"Salt, sugar if possible. Vitamins, and above all quinine. There was another malaria attack last week," she added. "Half the comrades are sick."

"Poor devils," murmured Patricia. "Go on."

"Pencils . . . the stock is exhausted . . . notebooks, machine-gun bullets . . ."

"Machine . . . no, Ling," Patricia said, suddenly serious. "No, dear, not machine-gun bullets. . . . Now listen to me." She pointed out that material aid was certainly necessary, but that it was essential to bring help first of all to the comrades' souls. And she developed her theme: the *soul* was her constant concern. "Look, Ling, I'd like to go with you next time and speak to them myself."

"You, Pat!" Ling said again.

"Why not? Wouldn't they listen? Perhaps. In any case, it's up to you to open their eyes." She applied herself to persuading Ling to reform her straying brothers; to bring them gradually to the understanding that it was inhuman and harmful to their cause to spread terror and to massacre the innocents at random, as they were doing. Ling looked at her in silence, increasingly affected by her benefactress. And when Pat said, "After all, you feel the same way—there is no feeling more sterile than hatred, and none so vile. You have learned that, Ling. You must love thy neighbor, isn't that right?"

The girl answered in a low, serious tone that reflected the sincerity of a fresh determination: "Yes, Pat, you must love thy neighbor."

"You love *us*," Patricia insisted, "you love us, Bernard and me, the way we love you, don't you?"

"Yes," Ling answered in the same tone. "I love you, Pat. I love you and Bernard." She hesitated another moment, then took out of her pocket the machine-gun charge Kim had given her, showed it to Patricia, and murmured in a voice that shook a little, "I'm going to prove my loyalty to you, Pat. . . . Pat, Pat, they want to kidnap Bernard. I'll stop them. I'm on your side . . . !"

23   Happy to be alive, savoring the warm, humid air of Singapore with every cell in her healthy body, saturated with the success of a difficult enterprise and the perfect accomplishment of an imperious moral duty, Patricia was rejoicing in her triumph over the powers of Evil, admiring Ling sitting opposite her on the restaurant terrace overlooking the city, where the Kebun Besar planters had gathered for their little party.

Ling was the source of this euphoria that caused Patricia to drink more than usual this evening, as if in celebration of a memorable event; Ling, dazzling in her evening gown; Ling, who yesterday had given proof of her definitive loyalty and her adherence to the laws of the Christian world. The new terrorist threat scarcely tempered her joy. She would find some way to ward off the danger. The two of them had made a plan already. Ling would report that she had not been able to exchange the ammunition charges, and that Bernard was on his guard. The rebels would give up their project. And in a month they would be leaving for France.

And even when she thought about this sudden danger which had so brutally brought Ling to her senses, she was not far from seeing in it an intervention of Providence. The battle was won. She could not look enough at the girl joking so happily now with Bernard, who seemed so gay himself. She complacently ran through the thousand details of her physical transformation; for Patricia they were the reflection of a spiritual metamorphosis that was her own creation.

At the party's start the other guests' reserve had contrasted markedly with the gaiety of the Delavignes. Robert Jourdain stared insistently at all three, and looked perplexed. Remy was sullen and scarcely spoke at all. As for Helene, the condescending amiability she affected with Ling scarcely concealed her jealousy of the girl. Nevertheless, after several hasty rounds of drinks before dinner, they had managed to reach a state of relative animation so that they seemed almost gay and rowdy among the groups of English people around them. When the orchestra began, the vigor of their conversations almost drowned out the music from time to time, and couples glanced at them with reproach before heading for the dance floor with all the stiffness of officiants celebrating the rites of a tedious ceremony.

An airplane that had just taken off flew over the city at low altitude. A gloomy silence fell over the terrace for a few moments. Helene remarked with a sigh that the plane would be in Europe in forty-eight hours, which was what almost every person on the terrace was thinking, with the same disheartenment. Patricia shrugged her shoulders and glanced knowingly at Ling, who smiled back.

Ling saw no reason for sadness in the airplane. She had felt relieved, soothed, almost lighthearted ever since confiding in her benefactress. Tonight, her mind excited by the champagne and the atmosphere of the luxurious restaurant, she scarcely remembered that under Kim's leadership a group of her former comrades was heading for Kebun Besar at that very moment, and that she had betrayed their confidence. When such a thought occurred to her, her lips trembled a little; not for long. Her conscience was quickly salved. Here the Cause seemed a strangely distant thing. Was her place really among those desperate men? She had developed a horror of violence. A betrayal? Who could hate these smiling, affable people? Had she changed so much? A glance in her mirror showed her the relaxed and serene creature she had grown to love. She stared at the people surrounding her, one after another. Remy lowered his eyes and blushed each time her glance met his, and she found his expression delightful. Robert, on the other hand, had been staring at her with a disconcerting insistence, but that also had a certain charm. Even Helene's antipathy and jealousy, apparent beneath all her kind attentions, produced a curious satisfaction. And lastly Bernard, whose paternal kindness manifested itself in some new way at every moment—how could she not be indignant at the thought that her former comrades were trying to destroy him? . . . They were all so *nice*. They overwhelmed her with such delicate attentions. . . .

Here was Remy who had just asked her to dance. She was so absorbed in her thoughts that he had to ask her again. She recovered herself and accepted with pleasure. She imagined herself in his arms, and according to the formula her mind tended to adopt this evening, after months of struggle, she discovered that *this was not disagreeable.*

"Happy, Ling?" Remy asked after a moment.

"Very happy." It was true. She was capitulating more and more to the sparkling wine, the music, the decor of white linen and little lamps that cast a gentle glow, the silk dresses revolving around her. In a low voice she repeated, with intense conviction, "Very, very happy."

"You know, I'm sad to think you'll be leaving soon."

He looked so disappointed that the desire to console him grew within her like a pressing duty. The sense of charity that had been awakened in her heart imposed a constant sympathy with the distress of others. She felt it would be wrong to despise his discomfort. Her eyes grew caressing, and she pressed a little closer against him. "I'll come back."

"You'll see so many new things, know so many other people. When you come back you'll be a different girl. You will have forgotten me. I think even the idea of this trip has changed you."

"That's not true," she protested, with an increasingly tender smile that managed to conceal the weakness of her conviction and intoxicate Remy completely.

"Ling, Ling, I'm happy only when I'm near you."

She attached no importance to the meaning of his words. She was scarcely paying any attention to him. She had learned to like the voice that flattered her this way for its own sake. She was indulging herself in the delicate pleasure of dispelling pain and distilling hope merely by the charm of her eyes and the grace of her caressing movements. She pressed still closer to the young man, raised her eyes toward his, smiled at him without seeing him, and repeated the phrase that was beguiling her dreams: "I won't say it's disagreeable for me. . . ."

"Oh Ling, Ling, I . . ."

"Yes?" Ling said, broadening her smile.

He grew confused, blushed, turned away his head, and stammered something about the way she looked.

"Ling, you are radiant tonight—even more than usual. That dress and those jewels have transformed you."

"They're presents," she said, glancing at the table where Bernard and Patricia were watching them dance.

"A very handsome couple," Patricia was saying.

"Hmm?" said Bernard inattentively.

"I said, Ling and Remy make a very handsome couple, dear," Patricia answered. "The boy is crazy about her, that's obvious; but I'm not so sure she's as interested in him. It's too bad."

He interrupted her nervously, reproaching her for her extravagant imagination. She protested and pointed out that Remy had a fine future ahead of him. Bernard himself often sang his praises.

"That's no reason . . ." he said ill-humoredly.

"Dear," she sighed, "I'm sure you're thinking there's something wrong because Ling is Chinese. And here I thought that you were beginning to shake off your dusty old prejudices."

And while Bernard seemed fascinated by the dancers, she warmed to the idea that for some time had been growing in her methodical mind. "Think it over a little. What she needs is a real love affair. That would be the ideal way to finish off our work. I hope with all my heart that she meets the right man. She deserves it."

After having announced this wish, she stood up and headed toward the floor with Robert. Bernard stayed at the table, still deep in his thoughts. Helene sat down beside him.

"Pat's right, you know," she said in a wry tone. "They're a very handsome couple. She's not bad at all, that little Chinese."

"Extraordinary," Bernard murmured between his teeth. "I've never seen her so lovely as she is tonight."

Helene looked at him curiously, then shrugged her shoulders and followed the course of her own thoughts half aloud. ". . . And that Remy is all right, too. I never noticed it before myself. It must be the change of air. You feel so far from the plantation here."

The dinner was over. After several skillful maneuvers, Helene had managed to get Remy to ask her to dance. Bernard was dancing with Patricia. Robert approached Ling and spoke to her in a less self-assured tone than usual. "Happy to be leaving soon, Ling?"

"Very happy."

"I . . ." He hesitated, as if uncertain, then continued while she lifted her eyes to meet his, not at all surprised to hear again the murmur of his caressing voice. "I'll be sorry to see you go."

She thought, "How nice they all are!" And made sure her expression would dispel the slight disappointment of which she was the involuntary cause.

Encouraged, he continued. "Oh, I know, we don't see each other often. It's not my fault. I've been waiting for a long time for a chance to talk to you."

"Yes?" Ling's eyes now reflected the pleasure she took in guessing what his next words would be. He led her to the floor and continued. "Sometimes I think we understand each other so well, the two of us. Right now I feel perfectly happy. Do you?"

"I wouldn't say," she murmured slowly, pressing against him, "I wouldn't say it's disagreeable."

They passed near Remy and Helene. Helene noticed that her partner was following the Chinese girl with his eyes, and remarked on it with a pout. "My poor Remy, I assure you everyone's going to notice it."

"Notice what?"

"That you're so interested in Ling. Oh, I admit she's very nice; but after all, it's not so pleasant for me."

Thus solicited, Remy had to show a little more concern for his partner. Which he did, first out of politeness, then letting himself be drawn into the game. When she wanted to please, Helene could be quite successful.

"My little Ling," Robert was saying, "when you come back from this vacation you'll have to come and see us much more often."

"I don't think Helene likes me very much."

"Helene has nothing to say about it," he protested. "Look at her . . . with Remy."

Ling watched the couple for a moment, and seemed frankly amused by Helene's evident stratagem. Her air of detachment reassured Robert and succeeded in turning his head completely. "Ling, Ling, you look so wonderful tonight. Your dress and that jewelry are so becoming."

"They're presents," Ling said. She was staggering a little when they returned to the table. Bernard, who had been watching them for a moment, looked disturbed. Suddenly he declared the place was terrible, that all these "ladies and gentlemen" with their stiff faces were terrible, and that they would be better off finding a place with a gayer atmosphere. Helene agreed, and they decided to finish their evening in a Chinese dance hall, the Happy World.

24   Outside the restaurant, the usual scene occurred. When they reached the three cars—they had driven to Singapore separately—Helene attached herself firmly to Remy's arm and cried out gaily, "We can't leave this little boy all alone. I'm going with him." Robert protested that he didn't want to go alone either, and stared insistently at Ling. But Bernard acted more promptly and pushed Patricia toward him. "You go with Robert, Pat. I'll have Ling to keep me company."

They drove off, only Robert and Patricia taking the most direct route to the dance hall. Helene led Remy through several out-of-the-way roads, and managed on the curves to fall into his arms so readily that soon he stopped the car of his own accord. After a long kiss she confessed that she felt so lonely, that she had been thinking about him for so long, and that he had made her very unhappy by being so interested in that Chinese girl.

"I was crazy," said Remy, embracing her again. She pointed out that they could scarcely delay much longer tonight, and added that she would be in Singapore next Sunday.

With Ling sitting silently beside him, Bernard was driving very slowly, following a capricious itinerary of dark alleys lined with flowering trees.

"It's not a matter of chance that I wanted to be alone with you, Ling," he said suddenly. "Tonight is not a night like other nights." Ling trembled with joy. Beneath the quaver in his voice, so different from usual, she had recognized the caressing murmur that had beguiled her in the restaurant and which, under this vault of brilliant flowers, seasoned the night with mysterious nuances. She did not move, but listened eagerly.

"I'm so confused, Ling."

He slowed the car still more and turned to face her. His heart was beating like a boy's as he noticed that her shining eyes did not turn away from his. He stopped the car and put his hand on her shoulder.

"Ling . . . I'm happy to have you here, beside me. Are you happy to be here?"

"I won't say it's disagreeable," Ling murmured. He caressed her hair with a tender gesture, trembled at her smile, and continued to murmur nonsense without paying any attention to what he was saying.

"Ling, little Ling, you're ravishing tonight. That dress and that necklace have made you into a different person."

"Everyone has liked them," she said simply.

Bernard's delight was overcast by anxiety and a touch of bitterness. He told her he had noticed: all the men were paying court to her.

"But it's not the same," he declared, his voice impassioned. "Remy is a boy—you saw how Helene hooked him."

"I saw," she murmured pensively, without seeming at all concerned.

"You deserve much better than that, Ling. You don't love him, do you?"

"He's very nice," Ling said.

Bernard's face brightened at this commentary, then darkened once again. He violently castigated Robert's intentions, which he had guessed at once.

"It's really unforgivable of him. A married man!"

"And Pat?" Ling murmured innocently.

"Pat?" He said nothing for a moment, frankly stunned. "Pat? . . . No, Ling, it's not the same thing at all. Pat is a good sport, of course, but after all . . ." He hesitated, choosing his words, not managing to express how he felt with much clarity. At last he found his reply, and in a tone of intense relief remarked, "After all, she's an American, Ling." Then he brushed her forehead with a sudden kiss.

She turned toward him to murmur softly, "But I'm Chinese!"

"Yes, darling, that's just it!" He spoke with triumphant vehemence, as if, after laborious searching, they had discovered together an obvious, luminous truth that explained and excused everything. "Ling!" He passed gradually and so naturally from paternal affection to a lover's caresses that she scarcely perceived the difference and was not aware of the moment when he took her in his arms.

"Darling," Bernard said, "we won't be separated again. We'll spend this whole leave in France together —just the two of us."

"And Pat?" she murmured again.

But he quickly quieted her scruples, and his own as well. His exaltation overcame every obstacle. Pat? Oh, he would find some easy way to get rid of Pat, he was sure of that.

He released her reluctantly from his embrace and they turned back onto the road to the dance hall. Along the way he spoke of his plans, of France, and of the wonders he would show her there. He was rich. Ling would have nothing left to desire: he would give her jewels, dresses—all far lovelier than this evening's. She scarcely paid any attention to these promises, but the gentle, ardent inflections of his voice communicated his excitement, and when the car stopped she threw herself into his arms again with a sudden impulse of gratitude.

Bernard got out first. Ling did not move, seemingly plunged in thought. After a long moment's hesitation, she came to a decision. "One second, I've got to put on my makeup again . . . No, darling," she insisted, as he was watching her delightedly, "I don't want you to watch me—I'm still a little awkward about it. You go ahead. I'll meet you at the door. Leave the keys, I'll lock the car."

He obeyed and walked away. She watched him through the window, and when she was sure no one could see her she reached down and seized Bernard's machine gun, which was kept in a sling on the side of the door. She looked at it a moment, her face transformed, strained, and removed the ammunition with a quick, knowing gesture. She took the blank charge out of her bag, still hesitating, and then clipped it into the weapon decisively. It took her only a second. She seemed relieved, quickly put on some more lipstick, smiled into the mirror at her satisfied reflection, and rejoined Bernard. Together they entered the Happy World.

An atmosphere of rowdy pleasure—laboriously obtained—filled the hall. Bernard was conquered by it the moment they crossed the threshold, and his intoxication was now complete. At each table resolute drinkers had managed to obtain from the alcohol whatever state of mind they desired. A tumult of conversation filled the air, interrupted by the Filipino orchestra whose musicians were tuning their instruments between the dances. The circle of taxi-girls surrounded the floor which was empty for the moment. Behind them crowded the vast numbers of drinkers and impatient dancers, among whom the hurrying waiters, their coats dark with perspiration, traced their irregular course. Here Europeans in evening dress mixed with Asiatics, visiting the dance hall, like the party from Kebun Besar, to finish off an evening that had threatened to grow dull elsewhere.

Helene saw them first and shouted and waved to make herself noticed. "At last! We were wondering what had happened to you!"

Bernard replied carelessly that he had had trouble with the carburetor. He sat down, shouted for something to drink, emptied his glass, and ordered another.

Patricia cautioned him, "Don't drink too much, dear. Don't forget, you have to drive us home tonight. There's no chauffeur."

But nothing could restrain his excitement. When Helene, who was staying in town for the night, remarked that the drive back to the plantation was very dangerous and that nothing in the world could get her out on those deserted roads at night, Bernard shouted triumphantly, "But there are no more terrorists now, Helene! That's all over with. Pat has made them all as gentle as lambs."

Everyone laughed and drank some more. The din of the dance hall increased. The orchestra began a tune that made all conversation impossible. There was a clatter of chairs, accompanied by shouts of joy. The couples crowded onto the floor, and Bernard felt moved to the point of tears at the sight of the little Chinese girls in their split skirts dancing cha-chas with such childish grace.

Patricia leaned toward Ling and shouted in her ear: "Darling, everyone's looking at you—you're a *succès fou!*"

"You're all so nice," Ling murmured. She seemed bewildered, and her hand went to her forehead. Pat grew worried.

"You're not tired? You look a little feverish. I hope you didn't drink too much!"

"Oh no, Pat. I didn't drink too much. Only . . ."

She hesitated a moment, leaning toward Patricia's ear now, and confided in a delighted voice, as if she had just made a wonderful discovery, "Pat! Pat! I think I'm beginning to love men."

Confronted with the obvious sincerity of this ingenuous impulse, which she had encouraged for some time and which confirmed the success of her enterprise, proving that Ling's heart had been touched by the grace as well as her mind by reason of such arguments, the American woman trembled with joy and clinked her glass against her protégée's.

"Darling, I'm so glad. I knew you would leave behind that little wild creature with her heart so full of bitterness. Our world, Ling—I've always said so—our world can only be saved by love!"

25   Kim was lying next to Sen in the tall grass of a hillside overlooking Bernard's bungalow, separated from it by a ridge. By midnight they had reached this point of observation commanding the side of the house where Ling's window was located. Behind them the commando comrades, lying on the ground, were awaiting their orders in silence. "There they are," Kim said.

The headlights brushed over the compact mass of the rubber trees. The car turned onto the road leading up to the bungalow, which was lit by its headlights until they stopped at the garden. They heard a murmur of voices. Lights came on inside the bungalow, which returned to darkness and silence once the door was closed.

"They're going to bed," Kim said nervously, "and they'll fall asleep right away. If Ling has been successful she'll give the signal soon."

Sen nodded his head without answering. Behind them the partisans were noiselessly getting ready, trembling with the emotion that always overcame them before an attack.

A long time passed. It seemed like an eternity to Kim. He shared in his men's excitement, and was also feverishly thinking of the double result of this operation. If the French planter was taken prisoner, Ling's work would be done. She could return to camp, and there would be no obstacle to keep them apart any longer.

The signal was a lamp Ling was to put in her open window if her mission had been completed and the way was clear. And Kim was sure Ling had succeeded. She had seemed rather depressed at their last few meetings, but he could count on her hard-headedness and her skill in such circumstances. His eyes hurt from looking at that dark wall behind which he could imagine her, impatiently waiting for the right moment, she, too, ravaged by her impatience to rejoin her comrades. . . .

"You're sure they won't try anything tonight?" Patricia asked.

"Nothing, Pat, if I don't put the lamp out. That's the signal. They'll leave at daybreak and wait for another chance. They trust me," she added, with a suggestion of bitterness in her voice. "At our next meeting, in a week, I'll tell them it was impossible."

"That'll give us time to think. It's time to go to bed now, dear. Tomorrow . . . today, I mean, we'll find some way to protect Bernard together, without his even knowing it. Only a month left, you know; and in a month we'll be far away."

"In a month," Ling repeated pensively.

Patricia kissed her and went into her own room, yawning. Ling went to hers, put on her pajamas, then sat down on her bed, her head in her hands. She needed to concentrate after this evening's confusion.

The return from Singapore had been silent. Ling, half lying on the back seat, was pretending to sleep, but really observing her benefactors: Patricia, serene as usual; Bernard driving fast with that mixture of virtuosity and control that hope and enthusiasm can give. As soon as they reached the bungalow, Patricia had proposed one last drink. Ling was sitting next to her on a couch. Bernard had stared at both of them affectionately, delightedly, and then, pleading fatigue, had gone to bed. The two women had talked together like accomplices, like sisters. . . .

Ling lifted her head, let her hands fall at her sides, and listened. No sound broke the bungalow's peace. Bernard had gone to sleep at once, that was certain. Pat too. Kim had calculated wisely: after a trip to town, the white planters fell into deep sleep. The alcohol dulled their bodies. She felt a strange sense of pride and superiority in noticing that her head was clear. She was the only person awake in the bungalow. She made certain by creeping into the hallway and listening at their doors to the Delavignes' regular breathing. She returned to her room, carefully closing her door and locking it. She was free to unleash events as she chose, in whatever direction she pleased. She thought for a moment more, then seized the lamp beside her bed and walked firmly to the window.

"It will be dawn in half an hour," said Sen.
"I know."

Sen trembled. Kim's voice had betrayed a terrible disappointment. For a moment he looked worriedly at his leader, without daring to question him. It was clear that Ling should have given the signal long ago, and the wall still remained terribly dark. He lifted his head to examine the sky and was about to make a remark when Kim's hand fell on his shoulder and squeezed hard. "Look!"

A white stripe cut across the wall below them. Ling's lamp shone like a star behind the half-open window. Kim remained stunned for a few seconds, fascinated by the light.

He quickly recovered himself. The next movements required all his clear-headedness. He stood up and turned toward his men. They had already understood and were ready. They started down the slope, silent and invisible. It took only a matter of minutes to reach the ridge. There, after having watched for a moment, they walked on toward the bungalow.

Suddenly Kim stopped. Sen, following just behind him, heard the sound at the same moment, the sound of steps on grass. After a sign from the leader the whole troupe stopped where they were. They had reached the level of the jungle trees. The sound grew louder. Someone was walking toward them lightly, but not trying to conceal his presence. The cry of a bird softly filled the night. It was Ling's usual signal. Kim, astonished, lowered his gun and replied in the same way. She rushed toward him. She was out of breath but spoke rapidly, without giving him a moment to question her.

"I came to warn you. I lit the lamp because I wanted to see you, but you can't pull off the attack tonight. The French planter is armed. I couldn't change the charge.

He's on his guard. He took the gun into his room and locked his door. I have heard it."

Sen looked at her in surprise. "Ling has said he was not on his guard."

"That's how it is," she insisted, turning away her eyes. "He has not let go of his gun all day. His door and window are locked."

Worried, Kim forced himself to think more calmly. Sen pointed to the sky, in which grayish streaks could already be seen. "We must attack now. The door won't hold out long against us."

"But the warning will be given," Kim said angrily. "He will protect himself. He will shoot. The *matamatas* will be awakened. There will be a battle, and we will not take him alive. We cannot take that risk. I have received specific orders."

Everyone looked at him, uneasy and hesitant, when Ling, who had gotten her breath back, declared in a serious voice, "Ling has an idea."

"Speak quickly, little sister. The day is about to break. We must get back to the jungle."

Ling spoke deliberately, weighing each of her words. "Ling has thought much about this whole business. To take the French planter alive is impossible. But Ling believes we can do better today. That is why she has made the signal."

"What is it?" Sen interrupted roughly. "We have failed because of you. What is there to do now?"

Ling did not show concern, and seemed to be thinking again. All the comrades' eyes were fixed anxiously upon her. She continued slowly: "We must kidnap the American woman."

And as Kim remained silent, astonished, she did not

leave him time for any objection. She had prepared everything in her mind and set forth her arguments with methodical haste, pleading her cause with a faith and authority that impressed them all.

"We must kidnap the American woman, I tell you. First of all the American woman is a more important hostage than her husband. Her government is very powerful and will force the English to exchange her for Ho. And then, it is easy. The American woman has no suspicion. She has no arms. At this moment she is asleep, her window is open, and her door is not locked. I can take in four comrades who will seize her in a blanket and carry her out without struggle and without noise. Her husband will hear nothing."

A considerable silence followed these words, time enough for the Chinese to measure the extreme shrewdness of the plan. It was Kim, who, after exchanging several words with Sen, expressed their appreciation. He spoke with the tones of fervent adoration that Ling's mind inspired in him, while the reassured commandos prepared to follow the girl's guidance.

"Oh Ling, Ling, we are all as stupid as elephants. Even our great leaders have not conceived a plan so simple. My little sister Ling is more subtle than a musk deer of the jungle."

26   Rawlinson was not succeeding in giving his whole attention to the dull administrative report he was writing. He lifted his head every other moment and remained motionless, his eyes on the grass beyond the window, where a Javanese gardener was nonchalantly walking back and forth behind a power mower.

"Have you tried to reach Kebun Besar yet?" he cried suddenly.

Mr. Kha appeared, respectful and diligent. "I have just done so, sir. Mr. Delavigne is not at his office, nor in his bungalow. He will be told as soon as he returns."

Rawlinson growled impatiently and looked at his watch. It was almost noon, a time when the plantation managers were always busy with paperwork. He tried to shake off his troublesome thoughts. It was becoming a mania: he found everything that happened at Kebun Besar peculiar. Bernard had every right to go for a walk on his own plantation. It was true that since Pat had been kidnapped they might expect anything.

It was the idea of this abduction that had been working in his mind for almost three weeks. The investigation had taken place, but had not completely satisfied him. Of course, since this morning, he had cleared up what had happened to Pat. The business was a common one, and yet in this case he kept finding disturbing elements.

Actually, there were reasons for his uneasiness. That Chinese girl, that Ling, who claimed to have heard nothing . . . It was plausible, after a night spent drinking —Bernard had said the same thing, and his word could hardly be doubted. A new fact, however, had come to light yesterday concerning this girl, and had reawakened all the police chief's old suspicions. An anonymous denunciation . . . Oh, he knew perfectly well how much faith to put in this sort of letter these days, when every personal vengeance could be served . . . all the more since this one was quite vague and elicited no proof whatever. Still, he wanted to talk to Delavigne about it. First, of course, he would tell the poor fellow the good news—Bernard had probably not slept for three weeks thinking about the horrors his wife was going through.

"You're sure you told him I wanted to speak to him about something very important?" he asked Mr. Kha again.

"I have said so, sir."

Rawlinson dismissed him with an irritated gesture and tried to get back to his work. He was not successful. Kebun Besar obsessed him. He furiously thrust aside the official papers and kept in front of him only the anonymous letter, written in Chinese, of which the subject was Ling.

At Kebun Besar the bungalow seemed quite calm. The garden was deserted. For fifteen days no one had worked in the flower beds. The *mata-matas* were sitting in front of their cabin, whispering in low voices. One of them occasionally indicated the house with a furtive gesture. Then all eyes turned in that direction, and they shook their heads with a dissatisfied expression.

Only the houseboy continued his chores with mechanical obstinacy, caressing all the living-room furniture with his feather duster. He stopped only when the telephone rang. It was the third time that morning. Without hurrying he picked up the receiver and answered the operator in Malay. "No, the *Tuan* not here . . . I do not know. . . . Yes, I will tell him when he comes back." He hung up . . . *Tuan* Rawlinson again? Something very important? Perhaps news of the *mem?* He glanced furiously at Bernard's room, shrugged his shoulders, and went back to his work. Sliding from one piece of furniture to another, he thought bitter thoughts.

All the trouble came from that Ling; he knew it. The *mem* was not frightened of this plague, although he had warned her. The *mem* was too good. Goodness was a foolish mistake. She was punished for it now. It was what always happened when people were too good. . . . He had been right to send his letter to *Tuan* Rawlinson. Oh, he had not told everything; that might have turned the police chief against the *mem* and against himself, too; but he had said enough so that the police would make an investigation. That was probably why

Rawlinson had telephoned. He would certainly find out the truth and rid the bungalow of this serpent.

He stopped again to contemplate the *Tuan's* bedroom with angry eyes. He was standing there, motionless, his face rigid, when the door was opened. Bernard appeared on the threshold, wearing a dressing gown. He looked at the boy, apparently embarrassed. As if caught out, the boy went back to his work. Bernard stretched, assumed a casual expression, and asked: "Did the telephone ring a few times?"

"Three times," the boy said. "Same thing each one. The *Tuan* Rawlinson asked to speak to the *Tuan*. To speak very important."

"You should have called me."

"The *Tuan* has said . . ."

"All right."

He picked up the phone, intrigued by Rawlinson's insistence. Suddenly he thought of Patricia and his face darkened. She had been completely out of his thoughts for several days. Certainly it was about Pat. It was unforgivable not to have thought of it at once. He had to make an effort to scold himself for his unconcern, and asked to be connected with Rawlinson, his mind shaken by contradictory feelings. The boy discreetly left the room, but remained in the hallway, his ears cocked.

"Well, finally. Listen, Bernard. The most important thing first. Good news. We know that Pat is alive and in good health, probably being well treated. . . . Yes, let me talk. She is a prisoner, but these bandits say they haven't hurt her. I'm sure it's true because they're negotiating for her release against one of their men we captured."

"Will they succeed?" Bernard asked in a worried tone.

"Of course they will. I'm very happy for you. The American consul has taken the matter into his own hands, and you know what that means. Pat will be returned."

"When?" Bernard asked in the same tone of voice.

"Of course I understand your impatience, old man, but when there are several governments in an affair of this kind, it can take a little time, you know . . . perhaps a week—maybe two; not more than a month, I hope. In any case, it must be a great comfort to you to know Pat is okay."

"Thank you."

Rawlinson hesitated a moment at the other end of the wire, embarrassed. Then he continued after a silence. "Now, old boy, there's something else. That Chinese girl you took in . . . yes, Ling. I'll have to question her again. Very seriously . . . You're sure of her loyalty? I know, you told me that, but I've received a letter about her. . . . Oh nothing, just an anonymous letter; probably a piece of libel. All the same, can I come by Saturday night? I only want to check up on a few things . . . for now."

"Saturday? Of course. I'll expect you. Good-by."

Bernard sat motionless for a moment, his forehead wrinkled. "Saturday," he murmured pensively. With an impatient gesture he asked for another line. When he was through talking his face brightened.

It was after noon; he was happy to be free of all responsibility. For several days now he had delegated the management of the plantation to Robert, as it had been agreed upon by the board that Robert was to run things during his absence. The thought of his long leave managed to reassure him altogether, and it was with a smile of pleasure that he returned to his room. From the hallway where he was hiding, the houseboy stared after him.

27   Rawlinson had been summoned to Singapore Saturday morning. He was attending a conference where the exchange involving Patricia was being discussed in secret when he was called to the phone. It was an emergency call from Kebun Besar—Robert Jourdain was speaking. He had tried to get Rawlinson in several offices and seemed quite upset. The chief of police jumped at his first words.

"What? Disappeared! Bernard too?"

"Not the same way . . ." Robert tried to get his story straight. He had gone to Delavigne's bungalow, a little surprised not to have had any news from Bernard for several days, and had found it empty.

"Empty!"

"Only the boy, his face sour like a Chinese when he's been duped and isn't likely to forget it, if you know what I mean. He told me the *Tuan* had been gone for two days; left with *missi* . . ."

"*Missi?*"

"Ling. I'm telling you what he said. Try to understand me, old boy."

"Look. I was supposed to be there this evening. Where could he have gone? Didn't you ask the boy?"

"Of course I did. He said: 'The *Tuan* say him left for several days in hills with *missi.*' With *missi,* no less! Besides, it was obvious the boy didn't believe a word of it. I thought it was so peculiar that I called all the hill stations in the district. There are only four. He hasn't been seen or heard of at all."

"What about the baggage?" asked Rawlinson, trying to reason calmly.

"Two suitcases. Impossible to make the boy say anything else. Maybe you can question him . . . I've given up. I thought I ought to tell you."

"Thank God for that. You've been wonderful. It's serious. Very serious."

"Serious? Let's not exaggerate."

Rawlinson was surprised by his tone, which betrayed complete unconcern. It was true that Robert was not up to date on the latest elements.

"Listen to me, old boy, I have some new information about that Ling. She's accused of being a terrorist agent. So you see what I mean! She may have been responsible for Pat's kidnaping, too."

"It's possible, of course."

"It's nice you can be so objective about it. But just think! If it's true, she's led Bernard into another trap."

"Ye-e-s," Robert said in the same skeptical tone. "Now you listen to me. I know I'm no policeman, but

I've had a little experience in this country too. You're in Singapore now, aren't you? Before telling all Malaya, I advise you to take a step that will cost you very little effort."

"What?"

"Check all departures for Europe these last few days."

"What?"

"You heard me. . . . After all, this is when they're supposed to go on leave. Perhaps he decided there was no good reason to put off the sailing date . . . Cynical? Good. In any case, I'm not leaving my office. I'll do whatever you want if you come out here for an investigation."

Rawlinson, after some hesitation, took Robert's advice and began his investigation in the passport office. There he learned enough to be reassured about Bernard's fate. Bernard had left for Europe with Ling two days ago. Their passports had been prepared for some time before that.

The employee who gave him this information heard him breathe an obscene oath as he rushed outside in a state of excitement scarcely appropriate to an official of the British police. He sent away the *syce* with his car and began to prowl the city streets at a pace that made other pedestrians turn and stare at him while he kept murmuring at regular intervals, "The swine!" It was only after half an hour of such eccentricity that his indignation subsided. Then, his policeman's good sense returning, he felt himself gradually overcome by an intense curiosity and by the irresistible desire to shed a little light on all the points in the business that were still obscure. He decided to go to Kebun Besar; but first, since he was in Singapore, he decided he had better question Ling's family a little more closely than before. After all, there was no hurry. The matter was hardly serious, as Robert had understood at once.

He found his car at general headquarters and asked for the assistance of a Chinese interpreter who might be said to specialize in delicate interrogations. With this man, whose skill he knew well, he headed for Ling's mother's house.

"Well?" Robert asked.

"You were right. They left together."

"For France?"

"For France."

Rawlinson had just reached the main office, driving straight from Singapore. The new manager of Kebun Besar, after having dismissed old Gopal for the day, looked at the chief of police inquisitively. Rawlinson's eyes gleamed like a bloodhound's on a warm scent, and he looked certain of discovering the whole truth at the end of the trail. The further he proceeded with his investigation, the more he felt he was uncovering a new aspect of the affair, an important aspect which had hitherto escaped him, which fascinated his subtle mind, and the singular character of which managed to hold his disgust in check. Still, from time to time a shadow of melancholy darkened his animated face.

"Two real swine," Robert murmured, to break the silence. He spoke with the lack of conviction developed by a long career spent below the equator.

"Just what I said to myself at first. Now I'm not so sure," Rawlinson said speculatively. "I've just spent two hours with her family. There are a number of points that had escaped me. I think I'm beginning to understand."

"More evidence?"

"No . . . a question of interpretation. I've been doing some thinking, too. I've been thinking about some of her attitudes . . . there are nuances . . . that's it, nuances . . . an atmosphere you have to get used to gradually, like in your French novels. . . . I can't explain it to you straight off—it's too hard."

He fell silent again. Robert realized he would get nowhere by insisting.

"I've had the boy brought here. Do you want to question him?"

"Yes, right away," cried Rawlinson, shaking off his torpor and beginning to speak feverishly. "I must be damned sure not to neglect the slightest detail. I need more to go on."

His attitude was certainly strange; such thirst for clarity transcended mere professional curiosity. He seemed able to recover his peace of mind only after discovering in all its fullness the profound significance of this incident and analyzing the complex of confused feelings on the part of all the characters. While Robert called the boy, Rawlinson went out to get the Chinese interpreter he had brought with him.

The man knew his business. He did not upset the boy at the beginning, apparently reserving the methods of intimidation until later. He began talking to him in Chinese with a familiar conversational tone. He interrupted himself now and then to give the boy time enough to collect himself, and summarized what had been said in English for his chief.

It was a good way of getting hold of nuances, to use Rawlinson's expression. Thanks to these, the picture gradually emerged from obscurity, its lines appearing not so much from the old servant's declarations as from certain of his intonations, his silences, and a way he had of squinting when a question embarrassed him. . . .

It was the evening of the very day *Tuan* Rawlinson had telephoned that they had left. The boy remembered very well. He had answered the phone himself three times during the day, saying that the *Tuan* was not there, according to his orders.

"But he was there?"

"He was there, sleeping in his room . . . with *missi*, of course . . . as on the days before."

This led to a question asked in the most casual tone. He replied that *missi* had come to share the *Tuan's* room two days after the *mem* had disappeared. Two days? Rawlinson discovered one of those significant details he was after. He exchanged a stealthy glance with Robert and jotted it down in a corner of his mind.

"And then?"

And then the *Tuan* had gotten up after all to speak to *Tuan* Rawlinson. The boy thought he remembered it was about the *mem*. Then he had stood, thinking, and asked for a line to Singapore. The boy heard the words "passage" and "airplane." That was all. Looking pleased, the *Tuan* had gone back to his room to find *missi*. He had closed the door.

"You didn't happen to hear what they were saying?"

Just by chance the boy happened to be sweeping the hallway at that moment, near the door. Without meaning to, he had overheard a few words.

"The *Tuan,* sitting on the bed where *missi* still lying, said *'ma chérie'*—he had called her that for several days."

"And she?"

"She called him *'Mon chéri'* too. *'Ma chérie,'* the *Tuan* said, 'good news.' "

He had told her that Patricia was in good health, a prisoner of the terrorists as they had feared, but that she would soon be liberated. There was nothing further to worry about as far as she was concerned.

"Is that what he said?"

"Yes, *Tuan,* and she answer, boy remember: 'You can't imagine how happy I am, Bernard *chéri,'* and the *Tuan* say again he would have been very upset to leave without being quite sure of what would happen to *mem."*

"God, what hypocrisy!" Robert cried.

"Perhaps not, perhaps not," Rawlinson commented in the same hesitant tone. "We still need a little more information. Let him go on. Down to the slightest details."

The boy seemed to be making a violent effort to remember and revealed that on the preceding days the *Tuan* and *missi* seemed very worried about the *mem* . . .

"Upset," corrected the interpreter, after asking a few questions.

"And it was the girl who handed her over to them, probably!"

"People aren't all of a piece," Rawlinson said again. "It fits in rather well . . . with her mother, for example."

He seemed to be dreaming aloud, and ready to give a

few explanations himself. Robert made an effort not to interrupt. At a sign from Rawlinson the two Chinese fell respectfully silent.

"Suffering and sincere pity—that is the impression I'm beginning to get. . . . An impression, you say? Yes, but based on facts. I'm a policeman. For instance, you didn't know that she had been to see her mother before leaving the country, probably forever? With him? Of course. No, let me tell you; it does me good. This woman, for several weeks or even months, had found that her daughter was behaving much better toward her. This has been made quite clear in her answers to Mr. Ha's questions—Mr. Ha is very clever," he remarked, turning toward the Chinese interpreter, who smiled—"Thus, at the early stages of Pat's adoption, Ling was hard, sullen, distant, scarcely said hello when she came into the house, and left it with a sigh of relief. She seemed to despise her family, to hate it. . . . Oh, I'm sure of it now, she was a revolutionary; she had learned the new catechism. . . . Well, afterward she grew softer, toward her grandmother too, whom she had scarcely looked at before. From one visit to the next she changed. She stayed longer. . . . For example: imagine, one day she helped them clean the house! She brought more presents, and better ones, that she got from Pat. . . . And in particular her way of giving them was no longer the same. . . . Treats for her little sisters, you understand? She played with them . . . that was not an attitude. The mother told about it in accents that could not be assumed. . . . Another example: once, Robert, once she brought her sisters aprons she had embroidered herself! You have to learn to see things by nuances, I tell you.

"And that last day, what obliged her to go and make her adieux? Merely this, old boy, that she was not a hardhearted girl. She wept, my friend, she wept, do you see it? She wept. The mother, who is not an easy target, I can assure you, was quite done in. Even the grandmother sniffled when she remembered the scene. She wept! Can you imagine that? An initiate of the New Order who professes the profoundest scorn of her past, her ancestors . . . And that's not all. The mother didn't tell us, despite Mr. Ha's diplomacy. A Chinese woman does not reveal these things. But after a few words from the children, and judging from their well-fed look, I gather she did not leave her family in penury. Make no mistake—her lover, in answer to her requests, was more than generous with her, extending Pat's charity a good deal farther. Do you begin to see what I'm getting at? Thanks to Pat she had found, little by little, the meaning of filial piety. It was quite simple. And then, if her new sensibility extended this way to every creature on earth, even the members of her own family, why would it not also have included her benefactress?"

"Now you're the one who's being cynical."

His chief falling silent again, Mr. Ha continued his subtle interrogation.

The boy had distinctly heard Ling ask: "Did Rawlinson ask about me?"

"Then the *Tuan* change his talk and say not a moment to lose. He speak very low, then laugh out loud and say 'Saturday!' *Missi* laugh too."

Leaning over, by chance, to clean the door, the boy had seen through the keyhole how the *Tuan* was ruffling *missi's* hair, both laughing and playing like children.

"Carefree happiness," Robert commented. "Children!"

They had dressed quickly. That was when Bernard had announced that they were leaving for eight days in the hills. The boy was to take good care of the bungalow. The boy had asked about the *mem*. The *mem* would come back soon. They would certainly be back before her. Then the *Tuan* had seemed to change his mind and had begun to write a letter for the *mem*, which he had left. . . . While he was sitting at his desk, *missi* had called the boy and . . .

"He gave you a letter? Where is it?"

The boy did not believe he had a right to refuse the chief of police, and drew it out of his pocket. As Rawlinson opened it the boy continued of his own accord in French. *"Missi* call me and tell put suitcases in car. Voice very hard. Since she take *mem's* place *missi* speak always very hard to boy. Boy not like."

Another nuance. Rawlinson shrugged his shoulders and read the letter. Besides being an admission of abandonment, it contained enough information to inform him completely as to Ling's story. "She was the wounded terrorist."

"I was beginning to suspect it," Robert said.

Rawlinson dropped the letter and began dreaming aloud again.

"It was too good a chance for Pat. She couldn't leave in the dark a soul Providence had delivered into her hands. I can see her now. She began to wrench her from the eternal damnation that lies in wait for the blind."

"I can see her too," Robert said thoughtfully.

They were leaning toward each other, dazzled by the new light being shed at each moment. After all, there had been other scandals in the country; this one was not going to disturb them. On the contrary, they seemed to be feeling something like admiration, as if both had been struck by the sudden revelation of an occult Power, a stubborn and crafty spirit which, to satisfy the requirements of its mysterious designs, did not hesitate to set human lives on the most preposterous paths. The marvelous as well as the irritating aspect of this Angel of the Bizarre is that its unaccustomed interventions were always marked on some surface or other by a claw that perfectly resembled the seal of Logic.

"What I'd like to make you understand," Rawlinson continued stubbornly, "is that Pat has succeeded beyond any reasonable hope in her project of reformation. She has *really* opened her strayed lamb's eyes to the light."

"When Pat wants to do a good deed, no one can resist."

"No one can resist *them*," interrupted the chief of police with a trace of melancholy, not indicating what he meant. "*They* succeed in all their enterprises."

"So you really think that Ling was touched by grace? That she developed new instincts?"

"Yes, I really think so," Rawlinson said. At that moment the telephone rang.

Robert picked up the receiver with irritation. He was annoyed with this intruder for interrupting his thoughts. It was his wife. Helene wanted him to know that Remy was taking her to the club, and that she would probably be home late. . . . If he didn't mind? At first he answered rather dryly. Then his voice changed. Rawlinson, interrupting his own thoughts, raised his eyes to look at the Frenchman's face. Robert's accent now expressed a great weariness, a disappointment tinged with melancholy, as he answered, "But of course not, darling, not at all." Afterward he gently hung up the receiver and remained silent under his friend's intrigued gaze. Finally, with no transition, he continued their conversation at the point where he had left off. "New instincts, yes. You must be right. The simplest explanations are always the true ones."

"One of us, that's what she became," Rawlinson concluded.

Robert rubbed his hand over his forehead, as if to shake off an unwelcome thought.

"You're right, old man. One of us."